JEZEBEL FOUND

BROKEN HALOS MC
BOOK 1

B.A. CHILDS

This is a work of fiction. Names, characters, places, and incidents are either the product of the author's imagination or are used fictitiously, and any resemblance to actual persons living or dead, busines establishments, events or locales, is entirely coincidental.

Jezebel Found

COPYRIGHT © 2020 by B.A. Childs

Cover art by Covers by Jo https://www.facebook.com/groups/coversbyjo

Editing by Purple Orchid Editing https://www.facebook.com/PurpleOrchidEditor

ACKNOWLEDGMENTS

To my daughter, who didn't laugh at me when I told her I wanted to do something I'd dreamed about for a long time.

Charlene Namdhari

You have the patience of an angel. We may not have met face to face, (yet), but I feel we are already friends. I have learned more from you than anyone.

    I APPRECIATE YOU.

TL Swan

If not for your realness, your videos, and your encouragement, I may never have had the courage to finish and publish this book.

Karen Harper

I thank your prompt editing, your chats and your suggestions. Semi-colons are still not my friend, however I shall use them when necessary. My thanks to **JB Hartnett** for connecting us.

Jo Clement

Thank you for listening to what I was looking for in a cover. Covers by Jo gave me exactly what I envisioned.

1
_____

"WHAT DID YOU CALL ME, FUCKWAD?"

"Ah, you fuckin' cunt, I'm gonna kill you," spits the poor excuse for a human being I currently have pushed up against the brick wall outside my favorite bar.

I hate that fucking word!

Not bar ... the C-word.

Nothing makes me angrier faster than being called the C-word, even though I cuss like a man.

Pulling off my mirrored Ray-Bans with my free hand, and placing them on top of my head, I run my gaze down his putrid body, wrinkling my nose and curling my lip as I do.

This guy is what people generically see in their mind's eye when they think 'biker'.

His dirty, brown hair hangs limp and unwashed to his shoulders. He definitely smells like he needs a bath; his clothes look _and smell_ like they need washing, and he is unshaven. A paunch hanging over the top of his filthy faded blue denim jeans, tells me he's too soft to be giving someone like me shit. He wears a leather cut on his back, but I am too close to read the rocker.

Contrary to the MC books I read there are not that many good-looking young bikers out there.

This moron's a little shorter than me, but most people are when you're five feet eleven inches tall. With his right arm twisted up behind his back, I have my razor at his throat, and his smarmy face is pushed into the brick wall.

I let out a heavy sigh. I am tired as hell. We've been on the road for days with little time to sleep.

We had tracked a little girl whose father had supposedly kidnapped her from her mother, simply to find out the little girl's mother was a lying bitch. The guy loved his daughter and wanted to see her, but the vindictive bitch that her mother was couldn't see past the fact her ex had moved on to someone better, so she was trying to convince the courts the father had been molesting the little girl. The dad was so frustrated he had not taken her back after a visitation, and that was when we were called in. Shadow tracked them to a little place outside Phoenix and after some heated discussions … okay, he may have received a beating before the little girl convinced us her mother was talking shit. After that we apologized, patched him up, then we talked him and his new girlfriend into coming back to sort shit out with the courts. I don't know what will happen, but I hope it gets worked out for the little girl because she is the most important person in that deal.

It's been a long damned week.

The asshole I currently have under my blade struggles, bringing me back to the present.

"Not if you don't retract that statement and apologize for calling us filthy names, you poor excuse for a human.

I should cut your fucking tongue out here and now." I sneer in his ear coldly, using his paunchy body against him and pushing his face harder into the bricks.

I nick his skin a little with the edge of the razor to show I'm not joking, and blood dribbles from the wound down his unshaven throat.

The metallic smell of it permeates my nostrils and I inhale it gladly.

"*Fuck*! I'm sorry, all right? I was fuckin' around. Jesus I can't say fuckin' nothin' anymore without someone crackin' the shits. *Leggo*," Fuckwad grunts.

"Now that's better. What's a body got to do around here to gain a little respect?" I quip lightly as

I step back and release Fuckwad's arm, preparing myself for what I already know is going to happen next.

As predicted, Fuckwad, *my nickname for this douchebag*, turns, spinning to my left and swings a roundhouse with his meaty right fist.

Expecting this, I duck, making a fist with my right hand, ready to swing heavy and hard, but I don't get to punch him as his body is suddenly thrown up against the wall again. A large hand covers Fuckwad's fist and there's a massive, muscled, tattooed, arm at his throat.

Rising to my full height I look up, *yes look up*, to see the guy attached to the arm that has Fuckwad pinned.

I can only see his profile, but man, *what* a profile. Everything I see from where I'm standing screams sex on a stick.

This guy is taller, *much taller*, than me, about six-foot six judging by our height difference. He has an A-line nose, high cheek bones and though I can't see his eyes, his dark lashes are long enough to be a girl's. A designer beard and moustache surround his lips, which are set in a thin line. His golden, blond-streaked hair is tied up on top of his head in one of those man buns. A vein in his neck stands out, and I think it may be more out of anger than straining to hold FW against the outside bar wall, as his jaw is ticking as well. Allowing my eyes to travel to his shoulders, then his arms, I note his bicep is larger than the top of my thigh and ropey veins stand out against sun-kissed skin. He is wearing a cut, but nothing underneath it, and it hangs open as he leans into his captive. Chancing a peek, I see a dusting of fine, light chest hair, defined chest muscles and a six pack which lowers to a V, which then descends into a pair of tight-fitting faded black jeans, clinging to long legs. He has a silver spike-studded, black leather belt on his jeans, and black motorcycle boots with silver buckles on his large feet. On each of his huge wrists he wears black leather, and silver spike-studded cuffs that match his belt.

If you imagine Chris Hemsworth and Charlie Hunnam's love-child, you'll get the picture.

"I see you swing at a woman again, Slimeball, I'll end you," the giant snarls contemptuously. "Now as you were asked so nicely, apologize, then get the fuck back to the motel. You're on cleaning duty for the rest of the week."

Giant Mo Fo, *I like to think these names up on the spot*, steps back and lets Slimeball, *I like my name for him better*, go.

"Okay, Ghost, whatever you say," FW gasps as he straightens up his clothes and runs his fingers through his dirty, stringy hair. "But cleanin' for a week? That's the whores' jobs, not us men."

"See now that's another of your many problems, Slimeball; you don't know when your behind. Shut the fuck up and do as your told." The GMF snarls, stepping back toward him.

"All right, *all right.*" Bringing both his hands up in a surrender position, Slimeball aka *FW*, turns to me and grunts, "Sorry *ma'am*, for being disrespectful."

He gives me a glare that says he's not really sorry, looks me up and down, spits on the ground near my feet and walks off toward where there are about ten motorcycles parked.

I watch as he walks away, rubbing his windpipe, and take note of the MC name on his cut as he does, feeling the hairs on the back of my neck stand up as I do.

There's a picture of a vulture with horns inside a double circle, and the outer circle has flames. The top rocker reads Satans Vultures, the bottom rocker reads California Charter.

I have knowledge of the club name. This charter is a long way from home.

FW slams his leg over a black and chrome Harley, starts it up, and backs it out. Before he leaves, he gives me one last contemptuous look, and raising his finger and thumb like a gun, points it directly at me, and pretends to pull the trigger. Then, spinning the back wheel of the bike, he creates a rooster tail of dirt as he guns the engine and speeds away from the bar.

I watch him leave.

When I turn back toward the bar, I'm about to thank the GMF for the help, and at the same time inform him I could've taken Slimeball down on my own, but he's no longer standing there.

I didn't hear him leave.

Maybe that's why they call him Ghost. On entering the bar, I look for my people, who I had told to go on ahead, when the dumb as dog shit biker decided to speak to us like crap.

They know I can handle myself.

Harmony waves at me from a table near the back wall, and Cricket holds up two Coronas to let me know she already has my drink covered.

I nod to let them know I see them, and as I walk to our table, I casually scan the room to see who else is here, so I can figure out if they are a threat to me and mine.

A long time ago, I learned to always know who and what's around me, to expect the unexpected, and always know where my exit points are. *The hard way.*

The Last Whiskey has been one of our pitstops for many years.

It's a lone two-story building, square in diameter, built from reddish brown bricks that the desert sand sticks to. Upstairs is the living apartment where the owner and his partner reside, while downstairs is the bar area. In its heyday it was a whorehouse, but there isn't enough population for that type of employment to make the owner any money these days.

Roadside bars in the Mojave desert barely exist anymore, and we have claimed it and this territory since the other MC left.

Now and then the odd biker rides through, mostly nomads.

Nomads are usually freelance bikers, at times, but rarely, affiliated with a club. Sometimes they drop in on our compound, giving us the courtesy of letting us know they are on our ground.

MC's generally give us more warning, whether they are going to be passing through on a run or on vacation. It's an unwritten rule, and if broken, can have deadly consequences.

This is the first time I've come across so many bikers from the same club in our territory since *his* club left.

This mother charter of Satans Vultures have given us no such consideration, so either they have a purpose here or they're looking for trouble.

Maybe they're passing through on business.

Maybe they're checking out the area to start a new chapter.

Maybe they're after what is *ours*.

That's a lot of maybes.

———

Woody, so called because of his prosthetic leg, owns The Last Whiskey and is ex-army. He's the same height as me, with dark chocolate-colored skin, a shaved head, and deep brown eyes. He has four-foot-wide shoulders, and biceps Arnie would be proud of, although his stomach shows he's not exercising enough anymore. Standing behind the bar, he looks happy as a pig in shit because his bar's full.

Meanwhile Woody's life partner, Stuart, or Stewy as we affectionately call him, is totally the opposite. He's about five feet two, thin, with skin as pale as a vampire, and is looking more than a little frazzled at having all this testosterone in one place.

"What's the face for?" I ask Stewy, as I sidle up

beside him. "Thought you'd be over the moon to have so many hard-drinking men and women in the bar, forking over money left and right."

Jumping then spinning around to face me, Stewy rubs his chest. "Don't sneak up on me like that, woman," he snaps. "You almost gave me a heart attack."

Stewy is a little older than Woody I think, as his hair is graying. It appears to have become grayer since the last time we were here. Its thick though and cut short enough that a hand run through it would style it for the day.

"I'm sorry, man," I apologize, trying to stop my lips from twitching, "What's your worry? That they might start fighting and wreck the place? There's a fight every time I come here, so what's so different about today?"

"I thought they left this area. These are Satans Vultures. I know you've heard of them." He begins to wring his hands together.

My eyes narrow as I watch his nervous ticks. Man, he's really worried about these dudes.

"Last place they were at someone was knifed," Stewy continues in a whiny voice. "They've killed people *I* heard."

"So has Woody," I deadpan.

"That's different and you know it. Woody was in the army and that's what they do," Stewy replies with his nasally whine.

"Okay, Stewy, you know Woody will have it all under control. We have his back, and if all hell *does* break loose, we'll pitch in to help break up fights. It'll be fine." I reach down and rub both Stewy's shoulders with my hands, trying to stop him from becoming distraught.

Drama queen!

Woody keeps a sawn off, double-barrel shotgun under the bar and a loaded forty-four pistol near the till, and he's not afraid to use them.

Those who live in remote areas like this, have to rely on themselves to keep the peace most times.

Stewy points over to the bar, where raised voices can be heard, and seem to be getting louder.

"And how are you going to handle someone *that* big?" he questions me.

2

I LOOK TO WHERE STEWY IS POINTING, TO SEE THE BIG guy who helped me with Slimeball aka Fuckwad.

Ghost, was it?

Seated on a stool at the bar, he has one hand on his beer glass which still sits on the bar, the other clenched in a fist on his lap, while another guy who appears to be not quite the same height as the giant, is going all shades of red as he yells in GMF's face. I can't make out what he's yelling about as the music from the jukebox in the corner is too loud.

The dude yelling has deep chocolate skin, a few shades darker than mine, long, graying dreadlocks and is wearing what looks like the same cut as GMF. His beard's in a long braid which almost reaches his chest. I notice he wears a white T-shirt, and a brown, cotton-checked shirt with long sleeves rolled up over the T-shirt but under his cut. Black skinny jeans, and dusty black biker boots finish off his attire. His arms, which bulge at his biceps, are tattooed to the wrists.

From where I'm standing, he looks to have a lot of patches on his cut.

He may be the VP of the Satans Vultures MC.

Or maybe even the President.

GMF's face appears blank the whole time he is being yelled at, other than the tick at his jawline. Even the spittle coming out of the other guy's mouth as he roars his dissention at him, doesn't cause a ripple. Their eyes are drilling into each other, and when the yelling ends abruptly, they keep staring at each other, as if one is waiting for the other to make a stupid move.

Breaking the stare down, GMF raises his glass to his lips, drains his beer, slams the glass back on the bar, stands up, says something I can't hear, and turns to walk away from the other guy. Toward me.

That's when I see the scar.

I hadn't noticed it outside because he was side-on to me.

Because he has his hair tied up in a man bun, I can see it plainly. It runs from the corner of his right eye, down his cheek, to his jaw line. It looks fresh, as if the stitches have recently been removed.

So maybe there *was* a knife fight at the last bar.

Is that where he was injured?

I realize he's stopped moving and is looking directly at me. My mind has a fleeting thought of familiarity, and I tip my head as I watch him. No, I don't know him, and I shrug to myself as I negate that in my mind.

His gaze rakes over me from my feet to my face.

I have on a navy-blue tank top, untucked, with my cut over that, tight black leather short shorts, and black motor-cycle boots. My sunglasses now hang from the front of my tank top, pulling it down enough to show some cleavage. I work out regularly and am damned proud of my body, even with the permanent reminders on it. As I take in the big dude's physique with my gaze, my abdomen has an unfamiliar tingling feeling, and my body suddenly feels warm.

Letting my gaze glide back over the scar on his face in the opposite direction, I find myself looking into ice blue eyes.

Cold eyes.

The tingling feeling stops.

Is he angry at me?

I didn't ask for him to step into a fight I was quite capable of handling myself.

As the jukebox finishes playing *You Don't Know Me* by Jax Jones featuring Raye, the guy at the bar yells in a thick accent, "Don't you walk away from your prez when he's talking to you, Ghost, get the *fuck* back here now"

GMF aka Ghost breaks the stare down with me and continues walking toward the door as if he didn't hear a thing.

Why do I feel the need to follow him?

Harmony calls out to me that my beer is getting warm, and the music begins again, so I resist going outside, and turn toward our table instead.

"See, Stewy," I say as I leave the little man, who lets out a rush of air like he'd been holding his breath, "It resolved itself."

I don't let him hear my own breath of relief, as I don't know if I could have stopped the big guy if he started throwing punches.

The other one would have been a piece of cake, *maybe*, but not GMF.

Sitting around our table are seven of the twenty-one people in the Broken Halos MC.

Harmony is at the forefront.

She has been with me since I found her at age fifteen.

I found her on the streets, after her mother died and she had run away from foster care. She was outside a café in Bullhead city, pulling a half-eaten hamburger from a bin. I offered her a hot meal, and she only hesitated a few moments before she followed me inside the café to a bench seat. As we chatted, I told her about myself, and that I was living with a motorcycle club on the outskirts of Las Vegas. *He* had told me I could bring friends my own age to the club and promised me they would be safe. *He* always tried to keep us safe until …
Admittedly, Harmony took a little convincing as she had been approached several times on the streets by pimps and she also worried about human traffickers. She did eventually decide to come with me after I promised her she wouldn't have to do anything she didn't want to, and if she didn't want to stay she'd be free to leave.

Harmony was about five foot three then. She's five foot six now, with an angel face, almost ethereal, flushed cheeks, round ocean-blue eyes, button nose and full lips. Long blonde hair, lank and dirty looking hung almost to her waist. She was too skinny but relatively clean, although her jeans were a little threadbare. They hung off her, as did the oversize red and green T-shirt she wore, bearing some Christmas theme.

It was May.

After our meal we left the diner for the place she had stashed her few belongings and packed them in her backpack. Her place was a short walk from the diner, down a dingy alleyway, in an abandoned building.

She was a little hesitant about climbing on the back of my bike, but she did it anyway, and as we rode, I had to shout to her to ease up on her grip several times, as I was finding it hard to breathe.

So much has changed since then.

Harmony has grown into a beautiful, confident woman, and is totally loyal to me and the Broken Halos MC.

I'm proud to call her sister.

With her new-found confidence is the ability to keep a level head and stay calm in most situations, which in turn calms others, so her road name Harmony suits her.

She is our mediator.

Harmony also has the ability to kill you without breaking a sweat, having trained hard right alongside me and the others.

The one thing I don't understand, is why she has to ride a purple glitter Harley.

Or why she named the bike Unicorn.

Next to Harmony is my VP, Cricket.

Cricket *loves* women.

She likes to cock-tease, but we don't hold that against her. What we do hold against her is when she gets stone cold drunk, she tries to turn us all into lesbians.

I don't mind sleeping with a woman now and then, and a kiss or two is okay, but they don't sexually arouse me.

I prefer my friend BOB.

Cricket is five feet four, but don't underestimate her. She is not called Cricket because she's short. Don't let those deep brown eyes or beautiful round face, short black wavy hair, pudgy little nose, and Cheshire cat smile fool you. Nor her large breasts and curves. She reminds me a little of Rizzo out of Grease, but shorter.

Cricket is her road name because she carries an Australian cricket bat in a metal scabbard on the side of her bike. One side of the bat is for beating without major damage, the other side can and *will* cause major damage, even death.

We met at a bar, a few years after *he* took me away and brought me to Nevada, following my grandmother's death.

One night I was sitting at a bar on the outskirts of Phoenix, feeling bored. *He* had taught me how to ride a Harley and I had taken to it like I was born on one. His club had business in Phoenix, and I had asked to go with him and the crew. I hadn't told him it was to get away from the handsy men in his club. As I wasn't in on the MC's business, he had left me at the bar with my fake ID, telling me to wait there until one of the brothers came for me, and to not accept drinks from strangers.

Cricket tried to hit on me. I explained to her I wasn't really into that scene, but I'd have a drink with her. No one bothered to even check if I was of legal age. Cricket agreed to sit with me, so we sat and drank and talked.

I discovered she rode a Harley as well, and other than her sexual disposition; we had a lot in common. Cricket thought the fact I lived with a motorcycle club was exciting. When I told her, I wanted to start a club of my own and shared some ideas I had, she immediately agreed and asked if she could be the first member. It was early days, and I hadn't yet formed the other club, but her enthusiasm for a club that accepted people as they were, not how society expected them to be, assisted me in the decision to run with it.

He had suggested one day that I should start up a motorcycle club of my own.

It was either that or become the old lady of one of his club's members, and I didn't want that.

Neither did he.

Leaving the bar together, we headed for our bikes. I had previously called *him* and left a message on his voice-mail saying I was heading back to the hotel we were staying at, and that I was with a friend, along with a photo of Cricket's ID so he wouldn't go all alpha on me. The protectiveness he exerted over me could be suffocating at times.

Cricket and I were chatting as we walked, and I wasn't paying attention as we passed an alleyway.

I was caught off-guard when I found myself suddenly knocked off my feet and dragged backward into the alley. Someone had their arm across my throat and under one arm while the other wrapped their arms around my feet so I couldn't drop and twist out of their grips.

When I caught sight of Cricket take off running, my first thought was she had set me up, and I became blind with anger.

Twisting my arm into a position where it was almost popping out of its socket, my hand found the first asshole's balls and I grabbed and twisted with all my might. He dropped me in surprise, or pain, and I banged my head on the ground, dazing myself.

"You fucking cunt," he growled with a heavy accent, "we're not supposed to damage the cargo too much, but

I'm gonna fuck you up for that, big time." His hand twisted in my hair, as he punched me in my face, causing my nose to bleed.

Still dazed from banging my head on the ground, the punch made my eyesight blur and I fought to stay conscious.

I knew if I passed out, I was finished.

I felt myself being dragged backward again, this time by my hair, *it was longer back then*, which hurt more than my face. The other dude had let go of my legs but was beside me on my right side with his big hands around my upper arm, and though I couldn't see properly out of my quickly swelling eyes, I thought I saw a third person near my legs, which were now helplessly scrambling in the loose gravel for a grip.

Unexpectedly, there was a sickening thunk sound, and second dude screamed like a banshee and dropped to the ground.

"What the fuck? You're fucking dead, you …"

Thunk!

"Oomph!"

Thud!

First dude went silent.

The hold on my hair let go, and I scrambled backward as fast as I could go, until I hit something solid. Reaching back with my hands, I discovered it was a brick wall and I used it to help myself struggle to my feet.

Third guy was close, and I crouched into a fighting stance clenching my fists, ready to strike. I still couldn't see properly, but I could hear footsteps moving toward me. I gasped for breath and my heart pounded so fast and loud I was sure third guy could hear it.

"Come get me, you prick, while we're face to face. It'll be a lot different to attacking me from behind," I yelled, trying to sound confident. My outer self may have seemed calm, but my inner self was screaming for someone to help me.

"Stop, it's me," came a familiar voice. "They're down, you're safe."

The woman from the bar, Cricket. She hadn't run; she came back to fight. I relaxed immediately, dropping my hands to my sides.

Shoving some sort of cloth in my hands she gasped, "Here, wipe your face. They really did a number on you, huh? Bastards. Are you hurt bad? Can you still ride?"

One of the guys groaned and I heard movement.

"Oh no you don't, cocksucker," my savior snapped.

As I wiped the blood from my eyes, I saw Cricket hit him several more times with her weapon, then proceed to use it on the other guy.

"They won't be doing that again," she sighed, "and we won't be having to look over our shoulders either. Let's get out of here."

We left the bodies in the alley and making sure no one saw us, made our way to our bikes.

"What did you hit them with?" I asked, while wondering if we should call the cops.

She showed me her weapon of choice, and my eyes widened even with the swelling, seeing her holding some kind of bat. It was flat on one side and had small sharp nails sticking out the other side, which were now matted with the hair and blood of the dudes in the alley.

"My dad made it for me when I told him I was being bullied and beaten at school. He said no one would be game enough to give me a hard time about it if I was carrying this. I loved my dad," she added with a sad sigh, hugging her weapon.

It was a slow trip back to the motel, as my eyes were swollen, but I didn't want to leave my bike. *He* was waiting when we arrived at the motel, so I introduced Cricket and told him what had happened. Some of the SV club members were dispatched to do cleanup at the alley.

Cricket and I became besties, and that is why she's now my VP.

I owe her my life.

3

We sit at the table in The Last Whiskey for about a half an hour, drinking beer, laughing, and joking, all the while keeping our eyes on the other group of bikers, when Lordy decides he wants to play pool. Everyone agrees that we will do a round robin which means each person has a turn to play the winner, as there's only one table.

Lordy is a sweet guy, gaining his club name because he has a body that would melt a shrew's heart. Almost five feet eleven, he's a little shorter than me, with Viking good looks, vivid green eyes that twinkle when he's drunk, and full lips. He wears what is called a tickler, *that little bit of hair beneath the bottom lip,* but the rest of his face is clean shaven. His left eyebrow is pierced, as is his tongue. Wearing short blond hair cut into spikes, *which suits him,* and a body that is tight, muscled and sun-bronzed attracts a lot of looks from the ladies.

Most women's wet dream?

Nope.

He's gay.

And married.

Lordy had been a Navy SEAL and joined *his* club after leaving the armed forces. In the aftermath of what happened, when the other SV MC members remaining decided to move on, Lordy joined the Broken Halos.

None of his other club members even knew he was gay, but I picked it.

Lordy himself didn't want to admit it until Tinker came along. It took a lot of fisticuffs and swearing and some broken bones. Tinker ran off and married a woman, but left her and came back, before both of them finally gave in.

Now they're married, and open about their situation, though they aren't really a touchy-feely couple in public, and neither of them gives off a feminine vibe.

When they fight, its full-on punches and kicks, but they work it out each time.

They are accepted for whom they are and are becoming more comfortable with their acceptance each day.

Lordy sets up the table, while Nitro picks out some cue sticks and chalks them up.

Nitro is about to break after winning the toss, when an unfamiliar voice drawls, "We'll be taking this table ladies, so y'all best be on your way."

I look up to see three of the Satans Vultures standing behind Nitro, looking her up and down as one of them reaches for her cue stick.

"I'm sorry, but we're about to have a round robin, including all of us, so you'll have to wait your turn like everyone else. You weren't using the table before," Nitro comments quietly as she moves her cue stick to under her left arm.

I keep a blank look on my face as I watch her do this. It's a signature move of hers. These guys need to back off fast.

Nitro is five foot six. She's a slim, *some would describe her as skinny*, woman of twenty-seven, with long black hair in a French braid hanging over her shoulder. If you didn't know her, you would think she was a cheerleader with her cute oval-shaped face, high cheek bones, deep brown almost ebony eyes, and a slight smatter of freckles over the bridge of her small nose, which nestles above cupid shaped, pouty lips. She wears tight faded blue jeans, black biker boots and a loose white T-shirt, tucked into her jeans at the front and hanging out at the back, with no bra underneath. Because she has small breasts, she can get away with it. Her cut is worn over the top of her T-shirt, which covers her nipples.

Two of the three bikers' chuckle.

They stop smirking and straighten up as the guy who spoke before, his name patch says Ape, growls, "As I said, we are fucking playing here, so … *Fuck. Off.*"

Harmony steps forward and tries to placate everyone, but the three SV's aren't cooperating.

Without warning, Ape pushes Harmony to the side, and grabs for the cue stick under Nitro's arm.

Big mistake.

The thing about nitroglycerin is that it can explode without warning. All it takes is a little shake.

Before he can seize it, Nitro places both hands on the cue stick as she brings it out from under her arm and flicks the heavy end up, so it catches the biker named Ape in his windpipe, then in the stomach, then in the nuts.

Wham, bam, no thank you, ma'am.

She is poetry in motion.

The cue stick is already back under her arm as if she hadn't moved.

Ape is bent over at the waist, and I think he's trying to work out what the fuck happened, and which part of his body he should hold, his throat, his gut, or his nuts.

"Ready, Lordy?" Nitro asks, as she calmly steps to the table as if nothing happened and breaks the pyramid of balls on the pool table.

The other two SV's take hold of their injured brother, one on either side of him, tucking their shoulders under his arms, and help him toward the bar's exit.

"You know this probably isn't going to end well." I sigh looking them all in the eyes as I do. "When shit gets real, we need to take it outside. I promised Stewy we would not wreck Woody's bar, okay?"

We are playing the fourth round of our round robin pool game, when Jinx gasps loudly.

"Shit!"

I turn to see what her problem is, thinking she must have spilled a drink on herself or something, and come face to face with the dark-skinned dude who was shouting at GMF before at the bar.

"You beat up one of my men," he grates out, his heavily accented voice rough, probably from years of drinking and smoking.

"Is that a question or a statement?" I reply, cocking my head to the side and keeping my face

blank.

Nitro moves herself to flank him, but I move my hand slightly, signaling her to stay put and silent.

"You want to start shit in this place? Haven't you

heard about the shit that went down at the bar at the last stop we had?"

"We heard. We also heard someone got knifed," I reply bluntly. We need to know why they're in our territory, and if they pose a threat to us, although being here is classed as a threat on its own merit. "And this place," I do quotation signs with my fingers, "is in *our* territory."

It's normal procedure or courtesy to let one MC know when another MC is going to be travelling into or through their territory.

Unless there's a reason, like they don't want anyone to know where they are. Wars have been started over less. This MC are not hiding the fact they are here, so maybe they mean no harm.

Or do they simply not see us as a threat?

Possibly he'll let something interesting slip if I engage him in conversation long enough.

"Why don't we sit down, have a drink and discuss some shit?" the Satans Vulture states, matter of factly.

Arching my eyebrows that he voiced what I was thinking, I nod.

"Why the hell not?" I agree, then turn to my friends. "You all keep playing while I chat with the *gentleman* here," making sure I emphasize the word gentleman.

As I saunter to a table near the far wall, I look back at Cricket and lift the left side of my lip, and wink with my left eye. She knows the signal and will be ready to bring down the house if anything unruly happens. Anyone else watching me would think I was being cocky, but with some of the work we do, body language and the ability to signal without words can save a life.

I sit at the table, with my back to the bar, showing I have no fear of putting my back to most of his men.

Thinking the SV will go to the opposite side of the table, so he doesn't have my people at his back, I am mildly surprised when he doesn't. The cocky prick grabs the chair next to me, slides it as close as he can without touching me, and sits his ass down, so that we are not only face to face, but mere inches apart.

While he gets comfy, I eyeball him.

He's probably in his late fifties, with long graying dreadlocks, and a full beard. His hair must have been as black as his beard once, which is also flecked with gray, neatly braided and tied with a red hair tie.

His face has small scars here and there, probably from fighting, and looks weather beaten from being on his bike in the sun and rain. He probably doesn't wear a long-sleeved jacket while riding, but I think the heavy tan is natural. His skin-tone is similar to mine, only a little darker.

In height, I'd guess he's about six feet one or two, not much taller than me. Handsome is not the word I would use for him, but he isn't ugly either, with his broad nose, which looks to have been broken a few times, his full, dark lips, and caramel eyes.

He has the same colored eyes as me, which I find a bit peculiar.

The old guy is wearing faded black, denim jeans that hug his thick, muscled legs, and black biker boots with spiked studs on the toes. I don't fail to see the toe blades he wears at the front of his boots. *There is a trigger switch at the heel that if banged on the ground extends a two-inch blade out from the toe of the boots.* Smart weapons. On his torso he wears a brown and white checked shirt open at the front, with a white T-shirt underneath that also hugs him. The T-shirt contours a well-muscled chest, and his abs show that he works out. His cut is worn over the top of his shirt.

He notices me looking him over, and gives me a smirk, looking me directly in the eyes when I look up.

"Like what you see, sweet thing?"

Wrong. Wrong. Wrong.

4

INSTANTLY MY HACKLES RISE.

"Do *not* call me sweet thing. Got it?" I scowl at him coldly, curling my lip. "If you want a 'sweet thing', then you're in the wrong bar. It may have been a whorehouse once, but not anymore. I am *not* one of them, and I am not into older men. What I *am* is the president of the Broken Halos MC, and I *will* fuck your shit up if you don't start showing me and mine some respect. This is *my* bar, and this is *my* territory, Gramps, so if you got something useful to say, say it. If not, the front door is *that* way. You and your Satans Vultures can *move the fuck on*."

Needless to say, I am a *little* touchy about some stranger calling me sweet thing. It's what the sweet butts were regularly called in *his* club.

"You be threatening me, woman?" Gramps, *the name suits him*, growls.

"Stating facts, bud. Take it any way you want." I'm not backing down, as this will give him and the rest of them the idea we are weak and vulnerable, and *that* we are not.

He lowers his voice, and leans forward, crooking his finger as he moves.

"I been hearing a lot about your little club. I don't think I heard of many female presidents before. Must say I'm intrigued," Gramps says with a slight smirk on his lips.

The accent, Jamaican perhaps? The way he drops his H's and says TH like T.

"Obviously, that must be why you didn't have the common courtesy of informing us you were going to be travelling in our territory. Besides, we are no *little club*, there are more than the few you see here." This guy is trying to rile me on purpose. I cannot allow him to think we are merely a few. There aren't that many of us, although we are not all here today, so we could be thought to be an easy takeover.

Bring it on, Gramps!

He locks eyes with me, then slides his gaze away to look at my crew, who are still playing pool. I know they're watching and waiting for any signal, then they'll be on this guy like white on rice.

"This is *our* territory, so what are you doing here? You know you should give another MC the heads up when travelling through their territory, and I was *not* notified." I am tired of pussyfooting around. My preference is straight talking, as life is too short for anything else, and I learned that the hard way.

These people are *my* family. *Every* person in the Broken Halos MC.

I may not have ever survived the shit I've been through without them. It's my job to keep them protected.

"Last I heard this was Strikers' territory. I tried to

notify him, but his number has been disconnected. He and I used to ride together until he went nomad then started the chapter here. I've been meaning to come and see how he was doing for a while now, but you know how it is. Life gets in the way. Way I heard it they weren't called Broken Halos either. It was Satans Vultures MC Nevada Chapter."

Gramps stretches out the name and must see me flinch and my breath hitch at hearing *his* name. Caramel eyes harden, along with his voice

"Whether you like it or not, likkle gyal you need us here. Word is, war is coming your way, and soon. You will need all the help you can get. We need to set up an alliance with yours and Striker's outfits, so shake the attitude and talk to me," he states quietly.

I sit back like I've been jabbed with a red-hot poker, although physically the man hasn't touched me.

Mentally though, he's thrown my brain into a whirlwind.

There's been one person in my life who called me that, and *he* is gone, along with …

I shake my head to rid the thoughts I don't want to deal with.

Schooling my features, I casually reach down, appearing to scratch my leg, instead slowly sliding my razor out from its hiding place in my right boot. As soon as it's in my hand, I calm a little, then I lean closer, locking my hard gaze with his caramel-colored eyes.

Who the fuck *are* you?" I grate coldly.

"A friend, darlin'," he replies gently.

"Why did you call me that? There was only one person who ever called me that, and … *You. Are. Not. Him.*"

"No, I definitely am not, darlin'. Striker is a friend of mine from way back, and last time I heard from him, he told me he had a lock on you. I don't know if he figured it out on his own or if someone else told him who and where you were, but last time we spoke, he told me all about you. He was setting up a meet so I could see you with my own eyes, then he stopped calling."

He told this man about me. Why?

He wanted me to meet this man in front of me. Why?

I don't know how to feel about that.

"Well, *he* isn't here now," *I don't want to say his name*, "and I don't need or want help," I finish confidently.

"Sorry, likkle gyal, I wasn't askin'. I was tellin' you. I owe my old friend big time, for lookin' out for you when I couldn't, but I'm not givin' you a choice here. If I'd been a better man, I would have been here a long time ago. But I am here now." Gramps' voice cracks a little as he informs me of this and his eyes glitter with what appears to be ... sadness? Pain?

"So. *Where* is Striker? I haven't seen or heard from him or any of the Satans Vultures crew. And why are you wearing Broken Halos cuts?" Gramps huffs.

"The Broken Halos are my MC, *that's* why we wear these cuts." Not that it's any of his business. "As for your friend, he is ... gone. So is what is left of his MC. They've moved on," I finish.

I still can't fucking say it.

"Who are you? I'm not going to ask you again." I can feel a chill taking over my body, and goosebumps rise on my skin.

The old man sits back and sighs. With a resigned look upon his face he runs his hand over the top of his head and states cautiously. "I am the National President of the Satans Vultures and *all* its chapters. My road name is Lucifer, but to you and you alone, it's Max or Maximus Leone. I believe I am your father."

My breathing stops, my eyes widen, and I straighten myself in my chair, feeling as if I've been punched.

My father?

What is this, a fucking episode of Star Wars?

"Oh, *fuck* no! *No, no, no!*" I growl.

Leaping from my chair so quickly it falls backward, I place my hand on this asshole's face using my momentum to push him backward in his chair.

It all happens so swiftly I've caught him unawares. He and the chair slam to the ground, his arms still at his sides. My blade is at his throat, and my brain is buzzing like its full of bees.

He chuckles.

He chuckles!

What the ...?

"What the fuck did you say? I don't have a father, *Lucifer*." I snarl his road name in his face. "I never did. I was the spawn of Satan. My fucked-up mother will tell you that. If you could find her that is," I add with a sneer.

Last time my mother was sighted, I was three weeks old. That was when she dumped my ass on Grammy's doorstep along with a plastic shopping bag stuffed with my belongings, and told her she could have me, because she didn't want Satan's child. Grammy asked where my father was, and my mother told her I had no father, that I was the spawn of Satan. These were the answers Grammy had for me when I asked her about my parents when I was older.

Lucifer aka Max hasn't even broken a sweat. He is laying docilely on the floor, with my razor at his throat, and me straddling him.

I hear movement behind me, but I am not shifting my stare from his. Without his eyes leaving mine, I feel his right hand move slightly, as if signaling someone, and all movement ceases. It's only now I realize the jukebox isn't playing anymore and the whole bar is silent and heavy with tension.

I'm not worried though, as I know my crew will have me covered.

"Calm yourself, likkle gyal, I am not here to hurt you, or lie to you. I believe I *am* your father, and I have been looking for you all your damn life, since the moment you were stolen from me and my old lady. The crazy woman who took you was not your mother, my *wife* was."

5

I step off Lucifer aka Max and get to my feet quickly.

My stomach hurts, and I feel as if someone sucker-punched me, as I try to drag air into my lungs. The bees are still buzzing in my brain and my skin feels clammy.

Information overload, and I'm not ready for it.

I'm telling myself to calm down, using the techniques I learned after ... after *that* happened.

I don't even want to think about that.

In through my nose, out through my mouth, rolling my eyes upward as I calm my frazzled thoughts.

When I finally refocus, what I see around me is like something out of a movie.

Several of Lucifer's guys have guns pointed at me, while several of my MC have guns pointed at them.

Behind the bar stands Woody, a blank look on his face, his hands out of sight. I'm sure I know why too. He has his sawn-off shotgun in his hands, but what I'm not sure of is *who* he has it pointed at.

Stewy, looking like a deer in the headlights, stands at

the till near where the pistol is kept, but I doubt he will pick it up unless Woody's in trouble.

It's a right little old Mexican fucking stand-off in The Last Whiskey.

Lucifer rolls to his side, and using the table to steady himself, raises himself off the bar room floor. Then, with a grunt, he bends down to pick up the chair, and once it's righted, he sits down on it again as if nothing happened.

Running a hand over his face, he looks around and raises his hands. "Okay, people let's not go off half-cocked. Put your weapons away. We were simply talking, weren't we, likkle gyal?" he says calmly, arching an eyebrow at me, negating to mention I had been seconds from cutting his jugular wide open.

"Yep. Nothing to see here, folks," I agree, signaling my people to put their weapons away. As they reluctantly do, I casually flick my razor closed and slide my hand down my leg returning it to its place in my right boot. I stand with both my hands raised to show I don't have any other weapons in them. "Like the old man said, we were simply talking." My curiosity is now aroused, *extremely*. How many times do you have someone tell you they are your long-lost father, your mother is not your mother, and that you've been missing without knowing it?

That would make anyone curious, *I* think. It has undoubtedly piqued my interest.

I seat myself on the same chair I had been sitting on when this weird conversation started, facing the deeply tanned man sitting in front of me, who has the same caramel-colored eyes as me, blow out a slow breath, and state calmly, "Alright *Prez*." *It's easier to say than Lucifer and calling him Max doesn't seem right.* "Why are you concocting this story? What's in it for you? I've been around for nearly twenty-six years. If you have been looking for me all that time, you need better trackers."

"How about we get the fuck out of here, go back to your clubhouse ..." Prez hesitates, his

eyebrows arched. "You do have a clubhouse, right? Then we can all relax, have some drinks, and discuss details." Prez sighs wearily. "It's been a long journey, and I'm not as young as I used to be. If you repeat that to anyone, I'll put you over my knee and spank your behind." He chuckles, smiling as if we are on friendly terms.

Not yet, we're not.

"Yes, we have a clubhouse, and as for your last statement, the last person who tried *that* stunt isn't around anymore," I deadpan, trying not to let the sadness show in my voice.

Prez wipes the smug smile from his face. As he's about to leave I continue, "I need to discuss this with my people first. How many members do you have with you? The big guy sent one of your crew back to where you're located, so you must have other members? Women?" I don't mention Slimeball aka Fuckwad or GMF aka Ghost's names.

We don't want to find ourselves outnumbered in case this is an elaborate takeover plan.

"We'll get some shit sorted, then we'll see where we're at. I'll send for them if, and when that happens. My VP will make some calls, let them know what's happening. They'll be all right where they are for the time being. It'll be the present brothers for now," Prez says with a shrug of his shoulders.

Well if he's not worried about them, then neither am I.

They are not my problem.

Yet.

My people agree on taking this back to the compound, where we have the upper hand if any shit hits the fan. Everyone finishes their drinks, then Cricket rounds them up and herds them out to their bikes as I say goodbye to Woody and Stewy, letting them know we are taking the other MC with us, and we'll see them on our next pass.

Stewy looks relieved that we're leaving, and the bar is still in one piece.

I tell the Satans Vultures prez to follow our lead, and we climb aboard our bikes, start them up, and follow our road captain, Shadow, along the highway toward Las Vegas.

Before we take off, my headset crackles and I hear Cricket's voice, "Is this a good idea, Jez? We don't know anything about these guys, and we're showing them to our clubhouse? What if it is a takeover?"

It was a good idea of Lordy's to set up headsets and microphones in our helmets, which means we can communicate with each other when riding. He came up with the idea, having had a background in communications before joining the Navy SEALs.

"Lordy's riding flank to cover our asses. Keep your eyes and ears open everyone. First sign of a double-cross take out the prez. Oh, *and* the big dude next to him," I add virtually as an afterthought.

I don't want to try and deal with *him* one on one.

We chat over our headsets as we ride, and Cricket constantly checks to make sure we aren't going to be blindsided by the Satans Vultures MC riding with us.

Everyone is giving their opinion on what they think is happening, except me. They don't need to hear that the Satans Vultures MC *National* president thinks he is my father until he proves it to me first. I don't think he has even told his own people, as they appear as intrigued as we are about what is happening.

6

OUR CLUBHOUSE IS IN THE MIDDLE OF BUMFUCK nowhere in the Nevada desert, far enough away from Las Vegas, and off the beaten track, so the cops don't come calling, but close enough so we can get supplies when needed and supply our goods and services to those who require them.

We have Wi-Fi, cell phones, electricity, and running water.

All the comforts of home.

Only, it's not a home anymore; it's where I sleep, when I *do* sleep. It hasn't felt like home since *that* happened.

The only real home I ever knew was with my Grammy, but then I was taken away by *him*.

Our compound is completely fenced off from the outside world, with an electric gate out front, and surveillance cameras all around the perimeter. The fences are also electrified and all of it runs off solar panels which cover the roof tops of all the buildings in the compound.

We have never really been attacked.

Infiltrated, but not attacked.

Best to always be prepared though, *he* had drummed into me.

The clubhouse was originally a roadhouse.

It's an old two-story weatherboard, which we all pitched in and restored. It had been deserted for many years due to lack of water, lack of money, and probably lack of human contact.

He had bought it for a song, and ran his chapter of his MC from it, but once he was gone, the rest of the MC went their own ways, not wanting to stay in this area.

I was *too crazy* for them they figured after what I did to prove I was worthy of being the Broken Halos' president. Oddly enough, *he* left the place to me. I had no idea until the chapter decided they were leaving; one of the older members handed me the deeds and titles to the buildings and land, along with an envelope with my name on it that I have never been able to bring myself to open.

Those few who chose to stay, became Broken Halos, and elected me to remain their president unanimously, even though I was a mental case at the time.

I couldn't even step foot inside this place sober, *or straight*, for a long time. I was in a really bad place. My club, no, my *family* helped me survive the aftermath, and restoring this place helped me cope a little better. It isn't perfect, but it is in a lot better shape now than it was back then, and in some ways, so am I.

The kitchen, which is on the ground floor, is huge, and has up-to-date ovens, a couple of dishwashers, *because face it who likes doing dishes,* and large rectangular cutouts along the front wall facing into the common room, a combined lounge-bar area so food can be passed through without having to keep walking in and out through the door. The common room is open plan. There are two pool tables on the opposite side of the room to the bar, a huge TV screen on one wall. An old jukebox Lordy found on Craigslist and restored sits beneath the TV. Lounges and a variety of seats are scattered around, along with some tables. I inherited the mismatched furniture as well. The wooden bar, made from old railway ties, runs along one wall, with several stools of various shapes and sizes along the length of it. Furniture gets broken when people lose their tempers and I'd rather someone break a barstool than a face.

A steel staircase at the back wall leads the way to the upstairs, where we built smaller bedrooms to accommodate more people. They're not fancy, but they are livable. We also put in a couple of extra bathrooms. There is a workout room as well, consisting of some specialized equipment designed to keep us in shape, and includes a dance pole. Amazing what one of those things does for core body strength.

Outside are several bunkhouses, also renovated, with locker room style bathrooms. We also kept the public toilet blocks. All together, we can accommodate up to eighty people comfortably, more if we have to. The

barns, of which there are three, have been fitted out for
the bikes, trucks, and SUV's, as dust storms can be
pretty intense, and sand can do a fair bit of damage to
them if they sit outside in the weather for long periods.
One barn holds our fighting ring, another leftover from
his MC. It was originally used for illegal underground
fights, but now we use it to spar with each other, or to
work out stress. When a button on the wall is pushed, a
cage lowers from the roof and encircles the ring so no
one else can enter except the combatants, and vice versa,
no one can exit.

I've made use of the cage once.

Underneath our main building is an area practically
as large as the space above-ground, where we do our
work. Tracer is already down there searching for information on the Satans Vultures MC California Chapter and
its members.

No one enters the basement area unless they have the
code, been approved and are trusted a hundred percent,
which is about two thirds of my MC. The newer people
have yet to show me they have our backs. Even though I
handpick most of them, I can be wrong occasionally,
though not often.

Various plants including sagebrush, mesquite,
Joshua trees and cacti dot the landscape inside and
outside the compound. Animal life out here is minimal.
Rattlers are found on the odd occasion, but I think the
electric fence keeps most of them out, and coyotes from
becoming too inquisitive. A few of the club women
planted some drought-hardy trees. There are succulent
beds at the front of the clubhouse, and more near two
headstones at the back of the compound, down by the
back fence. Flowers don't fare well in the desert.

I haven't visited those headstones since they were erected. It's not as if there are actual bodies buried there; it's more of a memorial.

Their ashes were scattered with the Nevada wind.

My hand goes unconsciously to my throat and grips the small vial I wear around my neck on a piece of black leather.

Except for the ashes in my vial.

"Hey, you okay?" Cricket asks softly from somewhere behind me, pulling me from memories I don't want to have. Memories I've tried to bury deep down, lock up tight, and swallow the key to.

"Yep," I sigh, popping the p. "Just contemplating why this guy thinks we need his help," I lied to my best friend.

"Well, let's get this meet underway, and get some answers, Jez," Cricket replies, linking her fingers with mine and gently tugging me along with her.

I know she didn't believe me about what I was thinking, but she would never call me out on it. Cricket is one of the people who helped me survive my downward spiral.

The Satans Vultures who have travelled to our clubhouse with their prez are shown where to put their bikes, and stow their stuff, as we have agreed to play hosts for the night.

Cricket, Harmony, me, and the SV prez, Lucifer sit on the various old chairs and couches lining the side verandah of the clubhouse, watching everyone get squared away.

"I could do with a cold beer right about now," Prez states.

"Gather your people, come inside, and we'll get the tap running. While they're enjoying a drink, you can enlighten me about how and why you think we need help, and we can decide whether we need or accept it," I say breezily, although that is not how I feel inside.

There is something huge brewing, and I feel in my bones that it's not going to be good.

Looking over at him, I notice the SV president's eyes narrow at my comment. His lips thin as he presses them together tightly, and I arch my eyebrows and scrunch my lips.

Hmm, maybe I shouldn't have said that last bit out loud.

Standing up from my overstuffed armchair, I step toward a side door and enter the building.

My mind is ticking over with what Lucifer has said so far.

Is he really my father?

Where has he been for twenty-six years?

Why did he not know where I was if I am his daughter?

Did he not *want* to know where I was?

Did he have any idea of the life I have led so far?

Did *he* know about Lucifer, and if so why didn't he tell me, or was *he* afraid I'd run?

Questions keep popping into my head, and I try to shake them loose before it explodes.

I really need some answers, and the only way to get them was to invite this motley crew onto my home ground, among my family.

The screen door slams as I enter the house.

———

Standing in the open room, looking up to the high ceiling, I silently asking for a sign that I'm doing the right thing, when a voice sounds from behind me.

"Praying?" The voice is soft and a bit gravelly, as if it is not used much.

I turn quickly to see Giant Mo Fo directly behind me. *Damn*, he's quiet. I didn't even hear the

door open and close. Or was he already inside snooping around?

I really need to take more notice. I should know better than that. This may be my compound, but there are strangers within our walls tonight, and I should be warier.

As I lock eyes with him, I get that same odd feeling I had at The Last Whiskey, of familiarity, but shake it off.

"Nope, stopped doin' that a long time ago." I pop the p as I gaze at him. "I'm wondering what to feed everyone tonight. It's not as if we can get a pizza delivery out here."

"I can cook up something if you have a grill; we brought food with us." He doesn't even wait for an answer before he pulls out his phone, hits a few buttons, puts it to his ear and says, "Dingo, get the food coolers out of the cage, and fridge it ASAP. We'll be havin' a cookout tonight. Yeah, I'll be cookin'. No, we *are* their guests, but they won't be waitin' on us." He barks the last part, running his fingers through his hair, brushing it back from his face. When he lets it go it slowly falls back into the same position.

While he's on the phone, I study him.

GMF's a big man, tall, muscular, and even with the

scar he is blindingly handsome. The scar adds a bad boy edginess to him. *As if he needs it.* The man bun has been undone, and his hair falls to just below his broad shoulders, and I have a fleeting memory of a certain fullback on the football team at the high school I had attended until Grammy died and I was brought here, but I push it away. His bulging biceps have colorful tattoos on them, weaving their way up to his shoulders, but the lower half of his arms are bare except for the black leather cuffs. His beard and moustache are well groomed and shaped, and he has perfect full heart shaped lips. His muscular chest gives way to a six pack, *this guy is so ripped*, and between the V running down to the top of his jeans, I see a straight, fine gold-blond hairline from his navel disappearing into his denim jeans. There are several tattoos at the base of his neck, that I can only glimpse parts of, under his cut, and I wonder what they are. To top that off, his low cut, faded black jeans fit him snugly, and there seems to be a pretty fine package stored in the front of them.

My lips feel a little dry and I flick my tongue over them, rubbing them together to spread the moisture. Those weird tingly feelings are happening again of their own accord in my lower body.

"Like what you see?" he smirks, as he ends the call and tucks his phone back into his pocket. His gravelly voice brings me back to the now, and I have to admit I feel myself blush a little.

Oh my *God*! What am I *doing*?

"I was wondering if you own a shirt," I deadpan, shrugging one shoulder.

His full lips twitch at my bold-faced lie. He totally knows I was giving him the once over.

I shrug and arch my brows while sucking in and biting my lower lip.

Meh, you can't blame me for looking at the scenery when it's worth looking at.

"Follow me and I'll show you the grill and stuff." Turning away from his smug face, I walk through the room, adding a little more sway to my hips as I do, and out the back screen-door. As I step outside, I catch him in my peripheral vision. He's staring at my ass.

Knowing this thrills me a little. A smirk crosses my lips and I drop my head, so he doesn't see that I know what he was looking at.

We have a great relaxing area out the back. There's a wooden deck, raised a few feet off the ground, and on it stands a kickass grill. A firepit is set in the center of the deck inside a round cutout, so that its lower than us when we're seated, for the cooler nights. It has a black wrought iron mesh fence around it, so no idiot falls in when they're drunk, *because, yep, that happened*. The seating consists of several Adirondack chairs, old couches, and arm chairs. Lordy and Shadow hooked up a sound system, so we can have tunes out here when we're partying.

A blond, curly haired guy about six feet tall strides out the back door carrying two coolers, one on each shoulder. He's wearing black leather pants, a bright blue T-shirt with a dolphin on the front, a leather cut with his MC emblem on it and black motorcycle boots. His face is weathered bronze as if he has spent his life outside. There's blond scruff on his square jaw; his nose looks like it has been broken once, and his deep brown eyes have a mischievous twinkle in them. He looks more like a surfer than a biker.

"I woulda come quicka if I'd a known ya had female company out here, Ghost. G'day dahlin'," he says, winking and smiling broadly. His teeth are brilliant white, nearly blinding. "How's about you an' me hookin' up, laydah?" He has a strange accent; one I have heard before, maybe on TV. "Afta Ghost here cooks us up a treat, you an' me could have a little fun maybe. You look like my type … female," he keeps babbling, arching, and wriggling his eyebrows at me in what he must think is a sexy, *come hither*, look.

I fake smile back at him. He obviously doesn't know who I am.

"That depends, dahlin'," I try to copy his accent, "on what you're offering."

"Drop the fucking coolers and go get the rest of the shit we need, Dingo. You can flirt with the prez when you've done your fucking job," Ghost growls, glaring at him, then turning his eyes on me. They are now ice blue again. Even in the short time since I met Ghost, I can see his eye color seems to reflect his mood. Good to know.

"*What? Shit! Really?* You're the prez of this mob?" He turns his incredulous stare from me to the giant with the glacial stare behind him. "You're shittin' me, Ghost. She can't be Lucifer said Str…"

"Shut the fuck up and do as you're told, asshole," Ghost cuts him off. He is most definitely angry.

Dingo sighs, both his hands raised up in surrender mode, his shoulders dropping as he blows out a breath of defeat.

"Sorry luv, oops, Prez." He truly does look sorry.

"It's okay, I accept your apology as formal introductions haven't really been made yet. You can call me Jezebel," I smile and wink at Dingo, liking his brazenness just a little.

I hear a growl and Dingo begins to move. "Okay, okay brother, I'm goin'."

Dingo disappears around the corner of the house, and I turn to find GMF has gone.

I hate the way he does that.

Everyone pitches in making salads and desserts to go with the grilled meat, and I'm sure our guests will enjoy their dinner.

The platters are strategically placed on tables throughout the room, and everyone helps themselves.

GMF sure can work a grill.

Our two prospects Hope and Luke, *they don't get their road names until they become patched members*, are serving behind the bar.

Cricket lost our rock, paper, scissors competition to see who pours the tequila shots for those partaking. She's doing that, while sitting on the bar in her low cut, barely there, candy pink cotton top, with a black lace bra visible underneath, trying to hold in her ample tits. Her higher than high cut, denim lowrider shorts show not only her stomach, but her curvy waist as well. If she opens her legs any farther, everyone will get a view of what's between them too as there is barely a crutch in them, and she's gone commando. She looks over at me, smiles widely and winks.

Cock-tease.

Some of the SV's are ogling her, probably squabbling over who will be bedding her tonight, which makes me smile, because as gorgeous as she is, no man will be getting near that pussy. Not *my* VP. Not gonna happen.

"I think that's the first genuine smile I've seen since we met," exclaims Max, stopping beside me. I've decided to call him that, *for now*. He's talking above the music and chatter around us. "I see you're not drinking, you worried about trouble? My people won't start anything here, they've been warned, but if any of yours do I can't predict what will happen then."

"My head needs to be clear for this meeting you came for. I'll relax once it's done."

"I'm ready when you are, likkle gyal. Let's get this over with and let the celebrations begin." He's getting ahead of himself with the celebrations part. He still has to prove he is who he says he is, and I am his daughter.

It also sounds like Max has already had a few drinks as his accent appears to be thicker.

Or is he pretending to be drunk to see if I'll relax and let something slip?

Paranoid much? You bet I am.

"Okay, let's go to the meeting room where we can have some privacy," I reply, schooling my features. He doesn't need to know we can record anything that goes down in there. That way we can review shit later and work out what can be gleaned from this *visit*.

7

THE MEETING ROOM, OR *CHURCH* AS WE CALL IT, consists of a round table built from maple, our club emblem and rockers carved into the wood in the center of the table top. It's surrounded by sturdy wooden armchairs made from the same wood. There's a scattering of other chairs around the walls for extra guests.

We are the only two people in here tonight.

Hope follows us in with a bottle each of Rum, Tequila, and a couple of glasses. She places these on the table in front of myself and Max, along with a jug of ice cubes.

Cricket comes to the door and gives me that *sure you want to do this alone* look, to which I reply by giving her the *I'll call you if I need you* look.

I know she's not happy about my meeting with Max in private. None of them are. They want to know what is going on. It's also not like me to keep things from them, but I need to know if there's any truth to the story Max is trying to feed me, and if not, why he is trying to make me believe this shit. Then again, even if he *is* being honest, why has he and his MC taken it upon themselves to be our saviors? From whom?

He obviously doesn't think we can fight our own wars.

On that note, why *is* there going to be a war?

We haven't started one, so who did?

The only person that tried to start shit with us is dead.

Cricket closes the door as Hope leaves. I know she'll ensure no one interferes unless there's trouble.

"Okay, let's start from the beginning. *Who* are you and *why* are you here?" I pour Max a rum, myself a tequila, pick up my glass, casually lean back in my chair, and cross my legs all while eyeballing him.

Max sits back and gets comfortable, swirls his glass of rum, and takes a sip. "Good rum." He looks down at his glass as if he's trying to work out something in his head, then slowly blows out a breath, looks at me and begins.

"I haven't *fully* told this to any living soul before, so bear with me, hear me out without interruption, then ask your questions. Okay?" His eyes widen, and his eyebrows arch a little as he looks deep in my eyes.

I nod my agreement.

"A long time ago, there was a Colombian princess, daughter of a big cartel king. He wanted to expand his territory, so he promised another cartel king that when his princess was old enough, she would marry the other king. This other *king* was twenty years older than her, and an animal. Loved to beat on women, torture them, bend and break them. She was terrified, and told her father she wouldn't marry this man, *ever*. Her father cut her off from everything and everyone after that. Virtually kept her as a prisoner in her own compound. He killed or got rid of anyone she looked like she was getting close to, even sons and daughters of his underlings. Still she swore the wedding was not going to take place.

"One night, the opportunity she was looking for came and she escaped. She ran as far as she could, changed her name, her hair, her clothes. Somehow, she stowed away on a boat, and remained hidden until she got off at Jamaica. With no passport and no identity papers she had trouble initially. Because she came from such a privileged family, she had never needed to fend for herself. I was a young man then, with my first motorcycle, and was having some fun, when this young woman ran into the road in front of me. Swerving my bike to avoid hitting her, I fell off, scratching myself and my new bike up. I was so mad. I grabbed her by the arms and started yelling at her. She was shaking so badly. She looked like a junkie. Her hair was messed and tangled, she stunk, and she looked like she hadn't eaten for a while. Then this girl, she passed out in my arms. For some reason I couldn't leave her by the roadside, so I picked her up, put her on my bike, and strapped her to me with some rope," He stops as I frown at him, then shrugs and carries on, "She was unconscious. How else was I going to ride my scratched-up bike and hold onto an unconscious junkie at the same time, huh?"

I motion for him to continue his *fairytale*. I have to admit, it is interesting so far, although what it has to do with me is yet to be established.

Max shoots down the last of his rum and pours himself another. I haven't touched my drink yet.

"Anyways, I take her to my home. My baby sister, she comes by as I get there. She is shocked that I have brought this street girl here, but she helps me get her inside. While I make some food, Maria, my baby sister, undresses the girl, gets some warm water and soap, and cleans her up as much as possible. That is when she sees the pure gold necklace around her neck. It had been hidden by her clothes. Maria says to me, she is no urchin. She is either a thief or a runaway. Until she wakes, we won't know. Worried the girl will wake in fright and try to hurt me or herself, Maria decides to stay, and we think it best to tie the girl down to the bed to be safe. It takes a few hours for her to wake, and I think she might have been pretending to still be unconscious, so I say loud enough for her to hear, *let me see what we have under these blankets*. Well, the hornets' nest, she stirs. This girl starts fighting with her ropes, but she doesn't speak a word, just looks me in the eye like she will kill me before she lets me touch her. Maria tries to calm her, telling her no one will harm her, that the ropes are for her own safety, as well as ours, and eventually she stops the struggle. We tell her that if she calms down and talks to us we might untie her, but we must know some things about her first."

"So, what's this got to do with *me*?" Frustration is setting in. I hate sitting around doing nothing. That's when thoughts and feelings start to creep in, and I don't like that. The busier I am the better I feel. I'm trying hard not to knock back this whole bottle of tequila, but it's looking good right now.

"Easy now, likkle gyal, we are a while from that yet. You need to hear this from the start, not the end or the middle, to understand. You agreed no interruptions, remember?" Max gives what I assume is a stern fatherly look.

Fuck knows if that's what it is, as I've never had one. *Apparently until now, that is*

I sigh, pick up the glass in front of me and take a shot of tequila. Hope should not have brought in the whole bottle.

Max pours himself and I another as I set the glass down on the table. I don't say anything, I grab some ice cubes from the jug and add them to the glass, pick it up and lean back. The ice will slow my drinking.

"Okay," Max begins again, "the girl tells us her family worked for the drug cartels, and due to something going wrong her family has been killed, and now they are chasing her to make sure the whole family is eradicated. She says she has been running for her life for weeks. Except for the necklace, and her perfect English, we probably would have believed her. I ask her about the necklace, and she becomes very pale, and for a girl with olive skin, that is no mean feat. She tells us it was a gift from a friend whose father is a cartel king, how she grew up close to this girl, but now the girl's father is the one trying to kill her. Maria and I argue over what to do. My little sister feels sorry for this girl and believes everything she says. After all we hear this sort of thing on the news a lot. It is not an unusual happening in Cuba and Colombia. There are always revenge killings for misdemeanors among cartel families and underlings. Me, on the other hand, I suspect there is a lot more to this story and am determined to get to the truth. So, I decide to make her trust me, fall for me, and then she will let me in, maybe. She tells us her name is Elida, she is eighteen years old, and that her family were all killed. Once we are certain she will not run, we allow her to be untied, and the first thing she wants to do is have a proper shower, so while she does that, Maria goes to her house down the road and gathers up some clothes for Elida. Luckily, they are both small but curvy young women. The only exception is that while Elida has what appears to be large breasts, Maria has very little. When Elida steps out of the bathroom …" Max takes a gulp of his drink. *Is he shaking slightly?* Then pours another one without ice. "She is a sight to behold, even with the dark circles under her deep chocolate eyes, and the lack of healthy color in her cheeks. Her hair is combed and braided over one shoulder, and Maria's dress fits her perfectly, showing off all the curves she has in all the right places, as well as her abundance of cleavage as her breasts are squashed into a bra also courtesy of Maria, and there are now sandals on her blistered feet …" Max's eyes go soft, and he takes a deep breath before starting his story up again. "That's when I know that no matter what the real story is with this woman, I will help her. My life was her life." He runs his hand down his face and I swear I see a tear in his eye, but he blinks it away and continues.

"From that day we were inseparable, and even though she didn't come forward with the whole truth about her life, we fell in love. I helped her get fake credentials, and we got married. We met up with some Satans Vultures not long after. They promised family and security, so we left Jamaica and I joined as a prospect when we arrived in California. I became a full member and eventually worked my way up to be the VP. Then Striker joined us. Being one percenter, we had a faster turnover of members than law abiding clubs. I was VP when everything went to hell. Elida's family found us. They had never stopped looking. I didn't know who she really was until it was too late, otherwise I would have taken her to the other side of the world to keep her safe. She thought we were safe.

"Elida was about five months pregnant, when a young girl came to the Satans Vultures as a club whore. She knew what she was to the club members, and that Elida was my old lady, but she kept trying to get her hooks into me, and it wasn't until it was too late, we found out why. Striker tried to distract her, and we thought it was working. Her name was Verita. She behaved a little erratic at times, but so did a lot of club whores. Some had addictions, some were a little lost, and some were there for the sex. Verita was very religious. She didn't quite fit the personality of the part she was playing. Elida was also religious, so when Verita seemed to stop her little games trying to get me to take notice of her, my Elida tried to befriend Verita. Elida had never had a real friend, so she thought everything was good. They began going to church together every Sunday. I would take Elida and Striker would take Verita. We would drop them at the church, they would go and pray, then they would walk across the road to a little coffee shop to eat and wait for us to pick them up. Then one Sunday morning Striker and I had some club stuff to do. A few of our *exchanges* had been tampered with, so our prez needed us to oversee this one, see if we could figure out who was interfering with our *business*. It meant we had to be out of town for a couple of days. Elida was eight and a half months pregnant by then, so it was agreed that our prez, Wheels, would take her and Verita to church in his truck, and pick them up after their usual lunch, as Elida couldn't be on the back of a bike by that time.

"Little did we know Verita was working for Elida's father. She had been brainwashed into believing that I had put a spell on Elida, that I was in fact, the devil incarnate, and I had coaxed her away from her family with promises and lies. This was the opportunity she had waited for. After church, they went to the coffee shop as usual, but when Elida needed to go to the bathroom, as you do when your eight and a half months pregnant, there were men from her father's cartel waiting for her. She would have fought them as well as a heavily pregnant woman could. They overpowered her and carried her out the back door to a waiting RV. Verita led the way. They took her to where her father was waiting at a local hotel. He was disgusted when he saw she was pregnant. With the shock of what was happening we believe Elida went into labor, but instead of calling for a doctor, they birthed the baby, using Verita as a midwife. They rang a hospital for advice pretending to be on the outer edges of town where medical help wouldn't reach them in time." Max stops. His breathing is hard and heavy, as if he's in great pain, and a tear runs down his grizzled face. He picks up the rum bottle and sculls it all in one go. After wiping his face on his sleeve, he takes a few deep breaths, and goes on, his voice getting quieter as if he is having to force the words from his mouth now.

"Wheels, our prez, had friends nearby, who called and told him what they had seen, when Elida had been carried out to a waiting SUV. They were thinking that Elida had gone into early labor, and that I might want to know. They thought the guy carrying her was trying to help, so they hadn't interfered. Luckily, Wheels' friends *had* thought to get the registration of the SUV, so he called a cop contact who got him the registration results immediately. The cartel guy who had rented the SUV had given his correct identity, and the idiots had taken Elida and Verita to the very hotel room where they were staying. With help from another contact, Satans Vultures had the hotel name within the hour, and were on their way to rescue Elida and Verita, not knowing Verita was in on the kidnapping, or what was truly behind it. When they got to the hotel, the baby was about to be born, so no one was expecting Wheels and our men. They took out the first cartel guy who was waiting downstairs and burst into the room where they found two other men and Verita busy with towels and stuff. My Elida was on the bed with a gag tied around her mouth, her hands tied to the bedposts, and her legs tied to the other end of the bed, keeping them open for the birth. *Bumboclaats*!" Breaking into his native tongue, *I think*, and rubbing his chest, Max goes all sorts of pale, *and for a dark-skinned guy that's pretty bad*.

"Max," I touch his arm and he flinches. His face is screwed up, and he looks at me as if he'd forgotten I was here for a moment. "Let's take a break, maybe get some food?"

In reality, I want to find out where I fit into this sordid tale of escape, romance, and kidnapping, but this man in front of me looks like he is in real pain, and I have been there.

"No chil'. I be wanting to get this out before I can't. Do you understand? I need to tell you before I put my walls back up and lock all this back in a safe place where I won't have to think about it or say it out loud again. This is the first time I have told the whole story to anyone, and it will probably be the last. But first, I need more rum."

The SV president stands, strides to the door, and on opening it yells for another bottle of rum. Someone delivers it to him and as he attempts to close the door, Cricket pokes her head in.

"Everything okay in here?" she says, looking my way.

She then glances at Max who is pacing back and forth.

"It's all fine. We'll be out soon," I say calmly.

I know she is dying of curiosity, but she backs out and closes the church door.

Once he has regained his composure and his seat, Max unscrews the lid off the rum, takes a gulp straight from the bottle and begins his narration where he left off.

"Wheels and my brothers tackled the two cartel dudes who were staring at my Elida's private parts, leaving Verita doing whatever the hell she was doing between Elida's legs. Suddenly there was a baby crying, and Verita was holding my precious baby gyal in her arms. Everyone was wrestlin' and punchin', and while they were preoccupied Verita cuts the baby's cord, wraps the baby up in a hotel towel, and races from the room with her, ignoring the fact its mother was crying for her baby. My Elida didn't even get to *see* her baby. One of the two men gets free from Wheels and my brothers, but they overpower the other one. Wheels untied my Elida, took the gag from her mouth, and covered her with a blanket. Her mouth and throat were dry from the gag and screamin', so he gets her a glass of water from the bathroom. She sips the water and cries for her baby, for me, for the lie she has held on to from the time we met. My Elida tells Wheels her real name is Edelira, and who her father is. She asks for him to find her baby, and to find me. Hatter, one of my brothers, chased after Verita, but she and our baby were gone.

"They presumed Elida's father had someone waiting for them outside, and that they are both now with him. Elida seems to still be in much pain as she makes Wheels promise to find our baby gyal and to keep her and me safe. He does just that. After he calls me and Striker, tellin' us what has happened and orderin' us back home, he begins to wrap Elida up in the blanket from the bed she has been tied to, when he realized it was sticky with something. That was when he saw the bed was covered with blood. Not knowing how much blood a woman loses when she gives birth, or whether they should still be in pain after the birth, he doesn't realize until it was too late that my Elida was hemorrhaging. Wheels called paramedics, but when he got to the hospital, they tell him they are sorry, but they could not save her, she had lost too much blood. When I get to the hospital I am told her body has disappeared. Still to this day we do not know who did this. I am too late to tell her how much I love my beautiful Elida, to say goodbye even. I didn't get to see my baby." His voice is so quiet I barely hear him. His head is lowered, and his gaze drops to his hands. "I went a little crazy, no, a *lot* crazy. I promised on my life I will find my wife's queffa, *murderer*, and I will find my chil', no matter how *far* or how *long* it will take me." Max drains the second bottle of rum without stopping, throws the empty bottle on the table and leans back in his chair. He looks at me with such sadness in his eyes, then he looks back down to his hands, as his shoulders slump and shake with the weight of his grief.

He suddenly looks much older than he did when we entered the room.

I look down at Max's hands and they're closed into fists so tight his knuckles are white.

"I have done things I am not regretful for and will do more given the opportunity. Blood has covered these hands and will again. To keep you safe." He mumbles practically to himself. "I promised my Elida I would not stop until I found you and you are safe. They will only get you over my dead body."

My eyes are damp with sadness for this man's story. I haven't allowed myself tears in public for a long time and I'm not about to start now. Laying my hand on his shoulder I speak placatingly, "I need some air, Max. Let me be for a while please. I need to process this, and you need a break." As I rise from my chair Max again raises his eyes to mine.

The sadness in them is suffocating me.

I feel claustrophobic.

I need to go.

8

AVOIDING EVERYONE, I MAKE A BEELINE FOR THE BACK door.

The screen door slams behind me as I burst out into the back area of our compound, and although the air is cool, sweat is dripping off me like someone has tipped a bucket of water over me. The need for something to take the edge off is screaming at me so loud it's all I can hear. My shaking hands cover my ears, and my breaths are heavy and uneven. Spots swim in front of my eyes and I can feel my blood thickening in my veins as my heartbeat thuds harder in my chest. The ground is not very level out here, and I stumble as I try to get away from my diagnosed PTSD attack, nearly falling.

It takes a few moments before clarity hits, and I realize I'm being held tightly in a strong pair of arms, and instead of face planting in the dirt, my face is pulled into a very solid chest, and the panting I hear is my own. I try to control my breathing, as I press my face into hard chest muscles. Warily I push my head back and

look up with blurry eyes to see Ghost looking down at me with … pity?

"It's okay, let it out. Breathe Jez, I got you," he says softly.

Don't let them see you like this, his voice whispers through my head. *You're stronger than this, you cannot show weakness.*

I concentrate hard on taking air in through my nose, out through my mouth, and my breathing evens out as I regain control of my feelings. The smell of leather, oil and spice waft into my sensory organs helping me calm.

Outwardly, anyway.

Inside I am still the broken freak I've been for some time.

"Thanks, you can let go now. I'm fine." As I regain my composure, I step back out of Ghost's arms, immediately feeling the coolness. I slide my hands into the back pockets of my leather shorts willing them to stop shaking.

Nothing to see here.

"That must have been some meeting," Ghost says in that quiet smoke and whiskey voice of his.

"Yeah, something like that, I'm not usually that clumsy or emotional. Must be around *that* time, you know?" I lie as I try to brush it off as the monthly hormonal thing, but I can't tell if he's buying it or not.

Do I care?

He means nothing to me or my club.

Ghost locks onto my caramel eyes, his gaze hardening.

It feels like he's trying to figure me out, see into my soul, and it makes me feel vulnerable. "You best check on

Max. He's had a fair bit to drink, and he might need some help." Deflection is my go-to when I'm unsure of myself.

He glares at me a little longer, then slowly rakes his gaze down my body.

"Yeah, sure." His voice now sounds a little pissy, like I've said something to upset him, and his eyes narrows slightly before he turns away and walks silently toward the back door.

"Hey." A soft voice sounds behind me as I watch Ghost walk through the back door flinching involuntarily as it slams shut behind him.

It's Cricket. I should have known she would follow me out here. She's my best friend, and she knows me well enough to tell when I'm upset.

"Hey yourself." I greet her, trying to get my feelings in check.

"So, how did it go? Did he tell you why they are taking up space in our territory? Are we going to have a problem with them? Do I need to bring out Boris?"

Boris is the name of her cricket bat, her choice of weapon. I know she is trying to bring a little levity to the situation. A smile tips up the corner of my mouth slightly and she knows she has been successful, sort of.

"Well, no we don't know yet. There is still a lot Max hasn't told me. I needed a break is all."

Why am I lying to my best friend and VP?

"Okaay." She draws the word out. "We're calling him Max now, huh? So how about I come with you and we get it out of him together? No man can resist a little girl time, especially two of them. It's every man's fantasy isn't it?"

Now I know she isn't buying what I'm offering.

"Cricket, thanks, but until I have the full story, I can't bring the club into it. It may be a pack of lies. It may be some elaborate plan to take over our territory, or it may be the not so simple truth. Until I have some proof, I will be taking this on by myself. I'm sorry if that hurts, but I am the club president, and I need to know the whole truth before I bring any of you into it."

"Okay, just know I'm here if you need me." The hurt shows in her big green eyes, and it hurts me as badly, but if I'm to remain their leader, I need to act like one. Their protection is my priority.

When I return to the meeting room, Max is slumped in the same chair he was sitting on when I left the room, elbows on his knees and his head in his hands. Ghost is kneeling on one knee in front of him. He's whispering something I can't quite hear and looking at Max with a sympathetic expression on his face. I can see without doubt that he respects this man who claims to be my father.

Max looks like he's done for the night. He looks up as I approach. His eyes are glazed and narrowed, and his jaw is slackening in that way when you have had too much to drink and too little sleep. I've been there.

"Let's call this a night. We can continue tomorrow, Max. I'm exhausted." I'm giving him an out. My body is in fact wound up like a spring, so I guess I won't be sleeping much. The exhaustion I felt when we pulled up at The Last Whiskey has fled.

"This is not over, likkle gyal. I did not come all this way to lose you again. Maybe not so much rum tomorrow, huh? I'm getting too old for this shit ..." Max is still mumbling as he rises from the chair and moves toward the meeting room door. As he exits, he turns to me, and looking me in the eye's states, "If you need proof, I will get proof."

With that he leaves, closing the door behind him, leaving me with the giant who has now risen to his feet, and is looking down at me.

GMF, *Ghost*, is not standing very close, but I can still feel the hairs on my arms rising, as if they feel a pull toward him.

"Has he told you what's going on?" I ask.

"Bits and pieces. Max holds a lot in. He can be a cold motherfucker at times," Ghost replies, running his fingers through his hair, brushing it away from his face.

Why do I want to do that too?

"Do you trust him?"

"With my fucking *life*." There is no hesitation with that statement.

"Should I ... the club ... trust him?" I'm hesitant with my enquiry. "We know nothing about him, or you guys." Now I'm trying to be tactful, while using my feminine wiles, *who am I kidding*, to wheedle some information, anything, to gain the upper hand.

"With *your* motherfucking lives. And if you want information, you get it from Max. It's not my story to tell." Again, Ghost sounds pissy. He runs his hands through his hair again as if frustrated. His eyes narrow, and his body language has gone from soft to tense.

Okaay.

I have officially succeeded in pissing him off.

Again.

Ghost storms to the door and leaves without looking back.

Screwing my lips together tightly, I huff out a frustrated sigh through my nose.

What is his problem?

9

THERE'S A PARTY IN FULL SWING WHEN I ENTER THE common room area. The pool tables are being put to use. Heavy metal music is screeching through the surround sound system, and people are talking, dancing, drinking, hugging, kissing *and probably fucking* everywhere.

The last time this place was so full, it was not with my club, it was … *his*.

Lordy and his husband Tinker are at the bar, drinking tequila shots, licking salt off each other's necks, and taking it in turns to suck the lime piece from each other's mouths. It's good to see them relaxed even though there are strangers under our roof tonight. Normally they don't show this side of themselves unless it's only the Broken Halos.

Cricket has resumed her seat on the bar, pouring the shots for them. She sees me and motions me over. As soon as I get there, she raises a shot glass to me with one eyebrow arched. It's the *do you need one* look.

I nod. She hands me the shot glass and I down it without hesitation. Fuck, I needed that.

Once I set the glass back on the bar, she hands me a bottle of water.

Cricket holds the bottle a little longer than necessary, causing me to look up into her green eyes, as she's taller than me when sitting on the bar. I know she's trying to assess how I am, and where my head is at.

Putting on my best fake smile for her, I jerk the water bottle toward myself, breaking her firm hold on it. I hate she feels the need to watch me constantly, to worry herself that I might go backward at any time, for any reason.

I did this to her.

I did this to me.

She should be able to relax and be confident in her president.

When shit fell apart, I offered up my presidency, but it was a unanimous vote that no one wanted to replace me, so here I am still. I feel like I need to prove to them I deserve it.

Later in the night I'm chatting with some of the club members, while kicking back on a big black leather lounge, when I sense something is off.

The hair on the back of my neck rises, and goose-bumps scatter across my skin.

Casually I search the room with my eyes, and lock my gaze on Ghost, who is standing near the bottom of the staircase that leads to the upper level, staring back at me. He leans back casually against the wall at the base of the stairs without breaking our stare down, crossing one leg over the other and folding his arms over his broad chest, causing his biceps to bulge even bigger than normal. That is not the reason for my bad feeling. In fact, I enjoy that he's watching me. It means he's not fucking anyone else. For now.

Where did that thought come from?

Ghost arches a brow, as if reading my mind, and a slight smirk touches his perfect lips.

He smiles? Well, smirks.

Again, where are these thoughts coming from?

It must be too long since I've played with BOB. Yes, that *must* be it.

Unwillingly, I break the stare down between Ghost and I then continue searching for the reason behind my strange feeling.

There.

Lordy and Tinker, are still at the bar where they've been most of the night, but their body language has changed. There are two Satans Vultures standing beside them.

The two SV's appear to be smiling, but Lordy and Tinker aren't. Lordy's body language says he is pissed off, big time, and Tinker's hands are curled into fists at his side.

Standing from the lounge, I casually walk over to where the four men are facing off, and as I get within earshot, I overhear the two SV's sarcastic remarks about my married couple being gay. They are provoking them on purpose.

Big mistake.

"So, who is the top and who is the bottom?" one of the SV idiots asks.

I think he's called Mouse.

"Nah, they're both bottoms. Get it?" says the one I

think is called Heathen, slapping his counterpart on the shoulder, and chuckling.

As I stop beside my brothers, I hear Lordy grate, "Why don't you come outside, and we can sort this?"

Shit.

"What? You gonna kick our ass? Or is that lick our ass?" Laughing like he's cracked the most hysterical joke, Mouse doesn't know when to shut his mouth.

"No gays gonna touch *my* ass. Never realized it was a Bear club. No real club would let gays join. You have to be a *real* man to be in a *real* club," Heathen states.

Heathen abruptly pitches backward as Lordy punches him straight in the face.

He deserves it.

Having read Lordy's move I step to the side to avoid going down to the floor with Heathen. Lordy stands over him cracking his knuckles, when I see Mouse move out of the corner of my eye. His left hand had been in his jeans pocket until now, and I see why. He has slipped on a pair of knuckle dusters and is mid swing at the side of Lordy's head when I stop him with a throat punch.

Mouse grabs for his throat and goes down to join Heathen on the floor.

"You didn't have to step in, Jez. I had a handle on it," Tinker grates. He is probably pissed that he didn't get to hit one of them.

"Sorry, Tinker. Instinct," I say, placing my hand on his shoulder. He's tense, but no wonder.

I look around to see other SV club members rushing over to see if their brothers need help and turn to face off with them.

My club members know we can handle this but are watching and waiting to see if we need any assistance.

They'll be right in the thick of things if we can't get it under control quickly.

"Right you two. Outside. Get on your bikes and fuck off. You're not welcome in this clubhouse," I state tersely over my shoulder. There, that should settle this.

"You broke my dose, you fuckin' fag."

I wince. Oh boy. Lordy hates that word. So do I.

"Okay Lordy, take him out the back. You have my permission. Teach him a lesson but don't kill him, yeah?" I give him the nod. We don't fight for no reason, but this isn't *nothing*. This asswipe needs a lesson.

Lordy grabs Heathen by the foot and drags him toward the back door.

"Aren't you gonna *do* sumthin', Ghost? Lucifer will kill these two for touching his brothers." Mouse gasps, still seated on the floor, rubbing his throat as I turn to look down at him. I didn't hit him hard enough to kill, just to drop him, although now I'm beginning to think maybe I should have hit him harder.

Really though, I'm not trying to make enemies here. At least not unless I have no other choice. Ghost is now standing so close to me I can feel the heat from his body seeping into mine. My body, *damn traitor*, seems to be enjoying it, as I feel my nipples pebble and harden.

What the ...?

He bends his long legs to squat down next to Mouse and cuffs him in the ears.

"This is *not* our house, Mouse. Lucifer made it clear there was to be no trouble here. You defied him and got sat on your backside by a *woman*. By the look of it, you're fucking lucky she didn't hit you harder. You could be dead right now. Be thankful you aren't. Do as you're told

and *get* the *fuck* outta here. *Now*. Go back to the motel.
Lucifer will sort you out later."

Ghost's voice, although appearing calm, is cold and
flat. Mumbling and grumbling, Mouse gets to his knees,
then his feet. He gives me an *if looks could kill* glare,
raking it up and down my body, spits at my feet, and
stomps out of the clubhouse.

Must be a club thing.

"Where did Lordy and that other guy go?" Harmony
asks.

Shit.

Moving quickly to the back door, I'm shocked when I
step out into the yard.

It's not what I was expecting at all.

Lordy and Heathen are sitting on a bench seat
drinking a beer, chatting like nothing has happened.

I'm standing here like an idiot, listening to them
chuckle and watching them clink their beer cans together
like old buddies.

Huh?

Heat encases my back and I know *he* is standing right
behind me again.

How?

I don't know.

"Well, I guess that's sorted." Ghost's voice is soft as
he places one large hand on my shoulder, brushing, *probably accidentally*, the side of my neck with his thumb. It
causes me to shiver.

"It looks like your man has a handle on this. You
cold?"

I don't want to move. I don't want to lose the heat
from his body, or his thumb from brushing my skin.

Why do I feel like this?

I don't even *know* this man.

"Nope," I reply as I make my decision. "Okay, what is going on here?" I move purposely away from Ghost and toward the two men, who are still talking and drinking.

Heathen stands up as I reach them and offers me his seat. He has obviously wiped the blood from his face on his T-shirt as it's covered in dry blood.

His nostrils are stuffed with tissue paper, and the skin under his eyes is already going black.

He didn't strike me as a gentleman.

"This here was a misunderstanding, ma'am. I'm sorry for causing a disturbance in your house. It won't happen again." Heathen looks me in the eyes as he says all this, as he plays heavily on his southern drawl, and I believe him to be sincere.

I frown in confusion.

"*Yes*, I did cause a fracas. *Yes*, I was being a total ass. *Yes*, your brother here is entitled to kick my ass well and truly. But when we got out here, he took off his shirt and I saw his service tattoos, and I realized how wrong I was. Turns out, if it hadn't been for SEALs, I would be a dead man now along with a lot of friends I fought alongside in Afghanistan. That deserves an apology, and my respect. I'm in his debt. Ooorah." Heathen raises his can to Lordy, and chugs down the last of his drink.

"And with that, I'm going to bed." Heathen looks at me, "That is, if I'm still a guest? I can understand if I'm not." He looks at me with one eyebrow arched.

"As long as Lordy's comfortable with this, I am." Our club is a democracy. If Lordy wants him gone, he's gone, just like Mouse.

"I can live with that." Lordy tosses his can in the bin and strolls back inside. Probably to find Tinker.

Members of both clubs wander back inside, some grumbling because they were expecting to see a fight, others because the party is still going, and they don't want to miss out on anything.

A strange feeling envelopes me, causing goosebumps along my arms. Rubbing them as if they're cold, I search the darkness beyond our compound but find nothing unusual.

"You okay?" I had forgotten Ghost was there.

In truth, no I hadn't.

"No, just tired. Time to fall into bed," I lie.

I rarely sleep.

Sleep is overrated.

The heat at my back disappears and when I turn, so has Ghost.

10

ASSURING CRICKET AND HARMONY I'M FINE, JUST tired, takes a few minutes. I know they worry about me; I wish they didn't feel they had to.

No. I *am* glad they care.

I'm glad *someone* cares.

Lordy and Tinker are ahead of me on the stairwell, holding hands, as they stride up the stairs, side by side. They're not normally as lavish with their feelings in public as they have been tonight, and I smile at the thought that maybe they are both beginning to feel comfortable in their own skin.

At least someone is getting lucky tonight.

It's not as if I couldn't get laid if I wanted to, I just … Oh who am I kidding?

If anyone tried, they'd find out how much of a broken freak I really am.

Besides BOB does a good enough job. He doesn't need his ego stroked. I don't have to feed him, or talk to him, and he's ready any time I am.

And he doesn't judge me, or care what my body looks like.

Since the refit of the clubhouse, I've taken the liberty of having the largest room upstairs for my bedroom. It has a large bathroom, with a spa-bath we confiscated, *along with weapons*, as payment when a dodgy client tried to back out on a deal.

I think everyone uses the spa-bath a lot more than me.

There is more than one bathroom, but this is the favorite.

I insisted we design and build it, so the bathroom has two entrances, one from my room and one from the room next door, that way I don't have to be disturbed when someone else wants to use it. The second bathroom entrance door is off another bedroom, but it's practically always empty. There's a queen size bed against one wall, with navy blue sheets, pillows and matching duvet, a dresser sits against the other wall, along with a tall cupboard. A small, frosted window allows some natural light. It faces the back area of the clubhouse.

I can lock the other bathroom entrance from my side to stop anyone unwelcome entering while I'm in there, the same as I am able to lock my entrance to the bathroom to stop anyone entering my bedroom.

The room is tiled with large, earthy, stone look tiles on the floors and halfway up the walls. The rest of the walls and the ceiling are painted white, so are the two doors. There is a double shower at the far-right end of the room, and the wall separating the shower from the rest of the room is the type of glass that if someone accidentally walks in on someone else having a shower, all they can see is a silhouette. There is a toilet behind a half wall, at the opposite end of the bathroom, and central is a white double sink with big silver taps. The same color tile bench that's on the lower walls surrounds the sinks, and it's set against the same wall as the toilet. Most of the wall above the sink is taken up by a mirror, tall enough that I don't have to bend to see my face. The spa-bath is set into the floor beyond the toilet.

What can I say? We like our comforts.

As I'm about to enter my room, Ghost appears behind me.

"I put Luc to bed. What happened in there? I know he can handle his alcohol better than any man in our club, but he's out of it. He only starts talking that Rasta shit when he's totally wiped. I can't understand a fucking word he's saying right now." His tone is accusatory, his eyes cold.

"That's his story to tell," I throw his words from earlier back at him. "And he's not my problem to deal with. He shouldn't guzzle two bottles of rum straight, like they're water, if he can't handle himself. I'm going to bed." I stop and turn to him, one hand on my door handle. "Oh, but what I can tell you is that Rastafarian is a religion, not *shit*."

Neanderthal.

Fuck you.

With that last thought, *or did I say it out loud*, I walk into my room and shut the door in his face.

My room is basic. There's a queen size bed beneath a square window, which has a heavy blackout blind on it. There is a tall, wooden chest of drawers against one wall, which is overflowing. Next to that is a cupboard for hanging clothes, although there's virtually nothing in there, except my prized signed book collection, the *Nine Minutes* series by my favorite author Beth Flynn.

You don't hang jeans and T-shirts up, so I don't have much else to put in there.

My limited shoe collection is thrown under the bed, along with a shoe box full of pictures I don't look at.

No. I *can't* look at.

There is one photograph sitting on my dresser. *The only one that survived the fire.* It's a photo of Grammy. Her gray hair is pulled back in an untidy bun, displaying the wrinkles at the outer edges of her beautiful dark eyes. The photo shows her flawless olive skin and her toothy white smile which is surrounded by large pink lips. She's wearing one of her many oversize shapeless dresses with an apron over the top and she's sitting next to me on her front steps, smiling at the anonymous photographer. Our arms are around each other's shoulders like best friends. I suppose in a way we were. At least I thought so. If Max is telling the truth, why did she not tell me herself? Didn't she know either? Or is this all an elaborate lie? If so, for what purpose?

With a sigh I deliberately put a halt to my thinking and keep my eyes and mind moving as I continue to peruse my room. I have a black comforter on my bed with a Broken Halos' emblem cover on it. A specially made present from my brothers and sisters. It's an enlarged version of the picture on our cuts. A skull sits centrally within the black, inner rocker circle. A set of white wings are behind and either side of the skull. Blood drips from the broken halo above the skull. Broken Halos appears in the top rocker and Nevada in the bottom rocker in black capital letters on a white background. Besides the comforter, a black fitted sheet covers my mattress, and four pillows with black BH matching pillowcases sit at the top of my bed. The bed itself is a wooden base with a high slat headboard at the pillow end, and the same slat end-board, half as tall as the headboard, is at the foot. Next to the bed on the right side is a chest of drawers with a black shaded lamp sitting on top.

Did I mention my room is full of black?

Like my life.

The top drawer contains BOB.

I remove my clothes and throw them into a basket in the corner. Hope says she's not searching for my clothes anymore when it's time to do the laundry.

When I was younger, I tried to sleep in a tank top and underwear, but every morning I would wake up naked, so now I just go with it.

The bed looks inviting, so I crawl onto it and lie down on my right side, with my legs bent at the knees. My eyes close, but my brain won't shut down.

Everything Lucifer aka Max told me keeps repeating itself.

Is he telling me the truth?

What is this war he speaks of?

Was my mother really his wife?

Did the woman who Grammy thought *was* my mother, Verita, mean I was Lucifer's child when she said I was fathered by Satan?

Maybe she believed he was the devil.

Maybe she was crazy.

Maybe they are *all* crazy.

If the woman who gave me to Grammy wasn't my mother, was Grammy my *real* grandmother? I think back to when there was just Grammy and me.

When I was younger, I didn't really understand why I had no parents. I had been with Grammy from around three weeks of age, so I knew no difference. It wasn't until I started kindergarten and began seeing other kids with a mommy and daddy that I started to question my life. Grammy would fob me off or change the subject or deflect my questions until I either forgot what I was asking about, or I would go sulk in my room. As I got older, she told me a few things; I guess she realized I wasn't going to stop asking. Eventually she told me about my mother leaving me on Grammy's doorstep with a bag of clothes and nappies and the words I would never forget, "She is the daughter of Satan." I loved my Grammy, and knew, *or did I*, she wouldn't lie to me, even if it hurt me. She loved God and didn't miss church unless she or I were too sick to attend. We didn't have a lot of money, or technical gadgets like mobile phones and computers, so we either watched TV for entertainment or played board games, or we sat and talked.

Grammy enrolled me in self-defense classes practically from the time I could walk, and I excelled. I had friends, but not really close ones. We had study nights together sometimes, but always at Grammy's house. I wasn't allowed to go to their homes. They thought it odd that Grammy wouldn't let me do sleepovers or have the latest technical gadgets.

I remember the one time I defied her and climbed out my bedroom window to attend a party my friends had coaxed me into going to. I was sixteen. One of my friends dressed me in her clothes and they all pitched in doing my makeup and hair, which was not easy to do when it was a mass of fuzzy curls. My hands shook with both fear and excitement at the thought of going to a party, and I wondered if our high school full back would be there. Perhaps he would take notice of me. Perhaps I would have my first kiss.

We hadn't been at the party long when an older guy approached me. He was good looking, with dark eyes, and darker hair. Tall, with olive skin, he dressed casually in jeans and a black tank with an unbuttoned flannel shirt over it and he spoke with an accent similar to Grammy's. I don't know if it was because I was nervous since I shouldn't be at the party, or because he was a stranger. I knew he didn't attend my high school, but I think my senses told me there was something a bit creepy about the way he kept trying to coax me away into the back yard so we could 'chat privately' as he put it. I politely declined his offer and remained inside, hoping my friends would see I was uncomfortable and rescue me. I had emptied my soda, I didn't dare touch alcohol, as being at the party was enough to get me grounded if I was caught, and the boy, really, he was probably more a young man, escorted me to the kitchen for another. He pulled a water bottle from the fridge and filled a fresh solo cup for me then guided me out of the kitchen.

Within minutes of sipping my drink I felt dizzy, and thinking it was the heat of the summer air and the closeness of all the people squashed inside the house, I excused myself, making for the back door.

I remember feeling ill and rushing for the fence line. The next thing I knew I had woken up in my bed at Grammy's with a cool cloth over my forehead and a very angry and hurt Grammy seated next to me. She told me a boy from my high school had brought me home, and he thought I had been drugged by an unknown person at the party. Grammy couldn't remember the boy's name. I was grounded for eternity, *that was Grammy's version of punishment*, but I knew she would eventually relent. Not that I wanted to go to any more parties. I couldn't even remember the name of the guy who was chatting me up, but he didn't fit the description of the one who brought me safely home. The next afternoon was when I met *him* for the first time.

He rode his motorcycle up my Grammy's driveway, and knocked on the door. Grammy behaved like she knew him and immediately let him inside. As he entered, he looked over at me as I lay on the couch still suffering from the night before, asking me how I was, and using my name like he knew me too. I remember thinking that was weird as I had never seen him before.

Grammy told me to stay on the couch and led him into the kitchen where I could hear voices but couldn't make out the conversation. At times it sounded like whisper-yelling and other times their voices were so low, I wasn't sure if they had stopped talking altogether.

Then Grammy and *he* came into the sitting room and Grammy introduced him as an old friend. She said he'd heard what happened the night before and wanted to ask some questions. At the time I thought he might be a cop. He asked and I answered as best I could, but after getting dizzy I didn't remember much. I described the guy I was talking to most of the night and saw his eyes narrow and lips press into a straight line, then he asked me the man's name and the weirdest part of that was I didn't know. I don't think he told me, but he knew mine as he spoke it several times, but I didn't remember telling him.

He rose from the couch and Grammy escorted him to the door where they talked quietly for a few more minutes, then I heard the motorcycle start up and he left.

I went back to school the next day and everyone asked me questions about what happened, and I hoped upon hope my rescuer would make himself known to me so I could thank him, but he didn't. Each day after that I felt like someone was watching me, from the time I left my Grammy's house to the time I arrived back. Sometimes, *though I told myself I was imagining things,* I thought I heard a motorcycle, but when I looked there was nothing to see.

He came to the house a few more times to see Grammy, and one night she told me that if anything were to happen to her I could put my whole trust in him, and if he told me to go with him, I was to do it, no hesitation. She didn't say another word about it, but I knew she meant it.

Three weeks later, while I was at school, she burned to death in our home. They thought she was napping when a candle caught on the curtains.

I had never thought about it before now, but Grammy didn't light candles in the day time.

I groan with all these thoughts that won't stop. My head is beginning to pound with an oncoming headache, so I roll out of bed and pad barefoot to the bathroom where I hope there is some Advil in the medicine cabinet. That is about the strongest medication I will find easily. Anything stronger will be under Nitro's guard, and I don't want to ask her for it, or let her know what's troubling me yet. Not until I'm sure this is not some sort of setup.

Leaning both hands on the bench, I look in the mirror and study the dark shadows under my eyes. Then I let my gaze wander over the reflection of my body. It's looking better than it was a while ago, I'm gaining back some of the weight I lost, I'm also gaining a bit of muscle tone with the weights and other exercises I've been doing. My breasts are average, but enough for my height and build, and they are still tight and perky.

My knuckles on my left hand are a little sore from punching Mouse in the throat, and I flex my hand to ease it. I am so far in my head I don't realize until it's too late that the shower's running.

My head turns at the grunt I hear from behind the frosted glass, and I see an outline of none other than Ghost. It must be him; no one else I have seen tonight is built like he is.

His body is side on to me, and I can just make out the contour of his face, muscled chest, stomach, and his ... *cock*?

Oh. My. God.

That thing looks huge.

It looks fully erect, touching his stomach, and even side on it looks thick, even if it *is* only an outline of it.

Trying to convince myself to creep back out of the bathroom, I find my legs won't comply.

I can make out what is probably his hand moving slowly up and down the length of his erection, and I can hear his breathing over the spray of the shower water. It's heavy, and ragged, as if he's on the edge. His hand moves a little faster, his breathing becomes slight grunts, then one hand plants on the glass wall as if he needs to hold himself up, as he makes a hissing noise.

Did he just hiss Jez, or am I wishing he did?

I squeeze my knees together and hold my breath as I watch this intimate moment. My pelvis pulls in like someone pokes it, my pussy clenches, and my butt tightens all at once. It's an unfamiliar feeling and I'm not sure whether it's good or bad as I've never felt it before.

Ghost begins to wash himself, oblivious to me being in the bathroom. When I realize I have just witnessed a very private moment, and start to feel like a creeper, I tiptoe out of the bathroom, having forgotten my impending headache, closing the door as quietly as possible.

I latch the bathroom door from my side. Crawling back into bed, I blow out a breath I didn't realize I was holding, reach into the top drawer of my dresser, and grab BOB, *my trusty battery-operated boyfriend*. I think I'm going to need him tonight, and boy do I have a vision to help me get off to. On the occasions I have imagined sex while I use BOB to get me off, all I have had is the clumsy attempts *he* made to help me, and the porn I watch on my laptop when no one else is around. Not tonight though. What I encountered has all kinds of strange sensations coursing through my mind and veins.

My hand slips under the covers and I turn BOB to high.

He barely vibrates.

Fuck!

Flat batteries.

FML!

No, no, no, not now, I whine inside my head, while beating BOB with my hand and turning the switch on and off a few times to see if it's a short circuit. *Dammit!* I need to release some tension, and my battery-operated bloody boyfriend is not cooperating. I throw him to the end of the bed, where he hits the wooden slats and bounces back to land between my spread legs as if to taunt me.

Frustrated but determined, I leave BOB there and get back out of bed, stomp to my chest of drawers, pull out a pair of old sweat pants, and slide them on, commando. I don't put a bra on under my tank top either. Then I trudge downstairs to the kitchen. If there are any batteries to be found, that's the most likely place they'll be.

It's the early hours before dawn, so everyone has either gone to bed willingly or has passed out, so downstairs is quiet, although there are a few snores coming from the lounges.

Heading to the kitchen area, I check every drawer with no luck. I slam the last one closed a little harder than I should then lean on the bench contemplating where I can find a torch, so I can steal the batteries from it, when I feel the hairs on the back of my neck rise.

I know he's there without turning.

My stupid body can feel him.

"Looking for something' particular?" Ghost's gravel voice gives my arms goosebumps. "Or can't sleep?"

"Can't sleep," I'm not lying, *sort of*.

I slowly turn to look at him.

He's standing in the doorway to the kitchen. His hair is still damp from his shower and it hangs down in waves. He has on his cut, no shirt, and the way his sculpted arms are raised above his head, holding on to the door jamb, I can see every contour of his chest and abs. His legs, slightly bent, and crossed at his feet, are clad in low slung, black faded jeans. The V at the base of his six pack points to what I now know is in the front of his pants. His feet are bare.

My eyes rove from his face, to his arms, to his torso, to his feet.

Even his feet are sexy.

Involuntarily, I feel myself blush.

What the fuck?

"I thought you might be having a little trouble sleeping after your peep show tonight." He chuckles and winks at me.

He knows I was there?

He knows I watched him stroke himself to an orgasm in the shower?

Goddamn!

That's embarrassing.

I blush again.

What is with this blushing bullshit?

I'm a grown ass woman, and I have to keep reminding myself that I'm the *president* of a badass biker club, so why am I blushing like some naïve little schoolgirl?

Matter of fact, I can't recall *ever* blushing. Until this man.

"You know you were welcome to join me for a closer look or feel." Ghost has moved so close to me there are only a few inches between his body and mine.

Like a magnet, my body pulls toward him without asking for my brain's permission, and my hands itch to reach out and touch him, but I curl them into fists and force them to stay by my sides.

"Seen one, seen 'em all," I deadpan, although my breathing involuntarily hitches as an image of him naked runs through my head.

I'm not going to tell him his is only the second of two naked men I have ever seen, *well kind of*, in real life.

"You keep telling yourself that." He chuckles again. It's a deep sexy chuckle, and I find it extremely hard not to smile. "I'm next door to your room if you need anything."

Ghost turns and disappears toward the stairs.

My body mourns the loss of his proximity as I watch him swagger away.

11

UNCURLING MY FISTS, I REALIZE MY FINGERNAILS HAVE broken the skin on my palms, virtually to the point of bleeding. I straighten up and take a slow deep breath in through my nose, and exhale out through my mouth, as I force myself to relax. My nerves are tighter than a spring, and if I don't find some batteries for BOB soon so I can relieve some tension, I feel like I'm going to explode.

Cricket sashays into the kitchen. *Is everyone having trouble sleeping?* She walks around me to the cupboard, reaches in for a glass, and proceeds to the sink to pour herself some tap water.

She drinks about half and extends the glass to me.

"Want some?" Her voice is a little croaky, as if she's just woken up.

"Nah, you finish it. I'm good." I push the glass back at her.

She purses her lips in that, *okay I will*, way, and finishes the drink. She then rinses the glass and places it upside down on the sink.

We clean up after ourselves here as much as we can, makes for less housework duties. I hung a sign above the sink some time back that reads in big black, bold letters, SOMEONE ELSE DOESN'T LIVE HERE.

That was the excuse every time the sink was overflowing or there was no milk, or coffee, or whatever.

Someone else forgot to buy it, or *someone else* must have eaten or drank it.

Now there's a roster for all cleaning duties, and although the newest prospects do the main stuff, we all pitch in to help maintain the inside and outside of the clubhouse.

Including guard duty.

"You on this morning?" I ask Cricket.

Dawn is breaking. "Yeah," she replies, stretching her arms over her head and yawning. "I better go get dressed." She begins to walk off, then turns to me with one eyebrow arched questioningly, "Why was Giant Mo Fo in here with you this early?" She uses my alias for him. "Did you two …?" She wriggles both her eyebrows and widens her mischievous green eyes.

"No, we didn't." I cut her off. "You know me better than that," I say a little sharper than I mean to.

"Shit, sorry Jez. I wasn't presuming, but I *was* hoping. I see the way you've been looking at him since he got here, and I keep catching him watching you. I hoped …" She shrugs without finishing her sentence.

"Yeah, well, other than watching him jerking off in my shower, there isn't going to be any interaction between Ghost and me, *period*." Too late I realize what I just admitted to.

A shit-eating grin fills her face, and she moves closer to me, grabbing my hand so I can't walk away.

"Oh. My. God. *You pervert*. Tell me more. Did you see his cock? Is he as big down there as I think he is? I know I don't go for men, but honey, you can't miss that thing in his pants. All the girls have been laying bets. Unless he puts socks down there. Does he?" Cricket's gushing like a little girl.

I can't hold back my smirk.

"In answer to your two million questions. I went to the bathroom looking for some Advil for my headache. I didn't realize there was someone in the shower initially. Then I saw his silhouette. Who else is that tall around here? He was masturbating in the shower, and to answer your other question, yes he is *that* big." I hold my hands out to show the length, then the width of what I saw. "*Fuck* is he big, *in more ways than one*. He could split a girl in half with that thing. I reckon even Butter," *one of the SV club's sweetbutts*, "would have issues with it."

Not that I want her anywhere near Ghost, or his cock. An involuntary shiver runs through me at the thought.

"Maybe he can use it as a weed whacker; there's plenty needs doing out there." Cricket giggles.

I'm now belly laughing so hard my sides hurt.

This is nice being able to laugh with my best friend.

"You need to get some of that, girl." Cricket joins in with me. "Lordy, lordy, lordy."

"Someone call me?" Lordy pokes his sleepy head through the kitchen doorway, with a quizzical look on his face.

His blond hair is mussed from sleeping, and his green eyes are dull, probably from the late night and early morning.

He must think Cricket and I have lost our marbles,

the way we are cackling like chickens, our faces tear-strewn.

Cricket looks at me, then Lordy, then laughs harder, setting me off again.

Lordy shakes his head in confusion and walks away mumbling something about "Crazy bitches."

There are no batteries to be found anywhere, so I wander off to bed, remove my clothes, and throw BOB into the dresser drawer. I must remember to get a bulk pack on our next shopping trip. It feels like I just dozed off when there's a sharp rap on my door. I grab my sweats and tank top off the floor, and stumble to the door in a daze, looking through the peephole. Cricket's standing there looking nervous.

"Yeah?" I grunt.

"Morning, sunshine." She knows I'm not a morning person. "Sorry to wake you Jez, but that guy you had the scuffle with at the bar yesterday? Slimeball? He's here. Says he's got a message for Lucifer. Do we let him in?"

"Give me a sec, I'll get dressed and be right down. I don't want that fuckwad on this compound unless it's absolutely necessary."

Cricket steps in while I throw on a pair of skinny jeans, a tank top, and my cut. I'm not uncomfortable with her watching me dress. She's seen my scars, before I had them tattooed over. Hell, she helped nurse me back to life.

When I'm ready, we descend the stairs together and head outside to the compound gates.

Sure enough, there stands Fuckwad aka Slimeball.

"What's the fucking *problem*? I need to see Lucifer *now*!" he demands. "Go get your fuckin' prez to go get *my* prez before I start some shit you'll *both* regret. Fuckin' women. Always gotta stick your *fuckin'* noses where they don't belong." He snorts back through his nose and spits a loogie on the ground.

I stand to my full height, crossing my arms as I do.

Dirty pig!

"Well, as I was trying so nicely to explain to you yesterday ... What was your name again? *Fuckwad*, was it? I *am* the *motherfucking* president of this club and you are *not* stepping foot on *my* compound if I can help it. So, give me your message and I'll relay it *if* I think it's important enough, to *your* prez, who I'm sure will be waking up with a giant hangover this morning."

Fuckwad points his fat finger at me through the gate. Oh, how I wish it were electrified right now. "You have got to be fuckin' jokin'. *You*? And the name's Slimeball. Get Lucifer now, or I'm comin' in there to get him myself. No bitches are gonna stop me either." Fuckwad snarls as he curls his meaty hands into fists.

"Slimeball. What the fuck, man? Ghost told you to stay at the motel with the others. What are you doing here? *And stop fucking yelling*!" Lucifer winces as he shouts at his brother. He sure does have a hangover.

As he strides up to the gate with only his jeans and his cut on, no shirt, and bare feet, I let my eyes run over him. For an old man he is pretty ripped. His hair might be going gray, chest hair included, but he's not one of these potbellied losers like FW here.

"We found Mouse this mornin', Prez. I know he was with you last night. His bike has been smashed to smithereens. Looks like it's been run over by a fuckin' tank." Slimeball looks genuinely sad telling this tale. "Mouse was by the side of the road near the motel. Doc can't tell whether he's been beaten to death or smashed by whatever did the damage to his bike. You need to come. No one saw or heard anything."

Cricket and I look sideways at each other without saying anything.

I only throat punched the little maggot; it wasn't enough to cause any real damage.

"*Fuck!*" roars Lucifer. He turns and yells to Tinker, who is standing in the compound having his early morning cigarette. "Grab my VP, tell him we leave in five minutes." Then he turns to me. "This better be an accident or we're gonna be doing some killing of our own when I find out who did this." The look on his face shows he means what he says.

He better not think any of us are involved.

Lucifer turns to march back toward the roadhouse, steps on a sharp rock, swears, and limps inside, still mumbling and grumbling.

"*Well?* You gonna let me in now, *bitches?*" Fuckwad snarls.

"Sorry about your buddy, but nope, not happening," Cricket says quietly. "You're not welcome on our compound. Especially with that attitude. When you find some respect, we *might* change our minds. You can wait for your prez right there."

We both turn and walk away, Fuckwad cursing at us as we go.

Inside, we hear Lucifer's men being roused. There's a lot of yelling and confusion.

"I'm going with them," I say quietly in Cricket's ear.

She looks at me like I'm crazy.

"Well if you are, so am I," she states flatly.

I would argue with her, but I can see by her narrowed green eyes and *taking no shit from you* face, there is no point.

I shrug and say "Well, we have about two minutes to get ready. Let Harmony and Lordy know what's going on and tell Nitro to get her ass on a bike quick smart. We might need her *experience*."

As I pass Lucifer on the stairs, I let him know we're going with him in case he needs fresh eyes and ears. He says nothing, but nods and grunts, as he strides to the front door.

The man is on a mission.

Something, or someone, just killed one of his own.

It's a feeling I'm familiar with.

Our saddlebags on our bikes are packed. Mine contains clean panties, a couple of tank tops and several weapons of choice. Cricket has Boris stowed on her bike, and Nitro is putting together her own version of must_haves. We roll out when Lucifer's road captain gives the signal.

Slimeball is not happy we're joining them. I can't hear what he's saying to his prez, but the dirty looks and hand signals he's sending our way are enough to let us know he's not agreeable to us being here.

I almost clip Slimeball as I ride past him to stop next to Lucifer aka Max, giving him the middle finger as I do.

He curls his lip and says something, but I can't hear him above the roar of the bikes, so I read his lips. Although 'love you' looks the same when reading lips, I'm pretty sure it's a 'fuck you'.

Slimeball and I are not going to be besties any time soon, but I don't think my heart will care.

I smile widely and move off with Lucifer, only the RC in front of us, everyone else falling into a two by two formation behind us.

Ghost riding at the back of the pack doesn't go unnoticed by me.

12

WE REACH THE MAIN HIGHWAY AND CROSS THE STATE line into Arizona. It takes about forty minutes to get to where the rest of the Satans Vultures MC are staying.

The town is called Nothing. It's mainly empty buildings, and an old motel that has seen better days. The old couple who own the run-down motel can't afford to leave as much as they can't afford to stay.

Nothing is about three hours from Vegas on the ninety-three, in Mohave County.

They probably appreciate the bikers staying here. It'd be the only business they'd get besides people who are lost, or those who want to get lost.

George, the old man who runs the motel, shows us to a cool room out the back of the place. It's where they've stored Mouse's body. The heat would do nasty things to it otherwise.

Nitro follows us.

She has a forensic science background, so she knows her shit.

When we enter the cool room, there's already someone in there.

The guy's tall, about Ghost's height, and built similarly. His thick mane of long, straight shiny black hair hangs past his chest. It's easy to see his Native Indian heritage. His unblemished tanned face is breath-takingly handsome, and his deep brown eyes are fixated on Nitro. He has a strong nose and full lips. There's a black and white bandana tied around his head, keeping the hair off his face. He's dressed in a black t-shirt with his cut over the top, black low-slung tight-fitting jeans, and black biker boots with silver metal buckles on them. His biceps bulge at the sleeves of the t-shirt and his huge arms seem tattoo free.

Nitro freezes for a fraction of a second when she sees him, a frown appearing, which doesn't go unnoticed by me, before she schools her face and continues on like nothing happened.

"This is Doc," grunts Max, not taking his eyes off the body on the slab. "This is Jezebel and Nitro."

Doc pulls his gaze from Nitro and looks to where I'm standing, grazing his eyes from my head to my toes and back again, then turns to look at Lucifer. His head cocks to one side, as if he's confused about something.

"This her?" His head jerks in my direction, his voice gruff but quiet.

"Seems so," sighs Max.

I look over and see Mouse laid out on a wooden trolley. He's shirtless, and his jeans are torn, dirty and bloody. His face is barely recognizable, and his upper torso is bruised, and dried blood is caked on his skin. After walking around the body several times, gazing down at it, Nitro turns away and dumps her bag on the shelf next to the table Mouse is laid out on with a bang, causing everyone to swing their gazes to her.

"Man has someone done a number on this guy. This is no accident." She comes straight out with it.

"What makes you say that? You haven't even touched him yet." Doc growls, scowling at her.

"Don't have to," deadpans Nitro. "See that bruise on his chest?" She points with her finger.

Lucifer nods.

"Yeah, that one. It's a fist. Several times. Heart punches. Someone knew exactly where to hit him to kill him. The rest will have been just to hurt him. Maybe they tortured him for information, but what would they be wanting to know that desperately?"

Nitro looks at Ghost, Lucifer, then at me, one by one. She seems to be purposely ignoring Doc. *Hmm … interesting*.

"Fuck. Looks like someone knows where we are and why we're here." Lucifer curses, kicking at the floor with the toe of his boot.

"*I* don't even know why you're really here, so how about clueing me in?" I narrow my eyes as Lucifer's gaze lifts from Mouse's dead body to mine.

I'm over this bullshit.

"You and me, Max. *Now!*" I move toward the door, and after a few seconds Lucifer aka Max follows.

Someone is dead.

I need to make sure this doesn't happen to any of my people. There's been enough death around me. I don't think I could survive another loss.

"Gather the club members for a desert burial," Lucifer growls back toward Doc before he exits the cool room.

Doc's reply is a nod and a grunt. Bad biker speak for 'Yep, on it'.

I walk away from the run-down motel and continue for about five minutes along a partly overgrown path, to ensure it's only Max and I, and no one else is listening to our conversation. Max's hot on my tail.

Finding a couple of flat looking rocks, with a three-hundred-and-sixty-degree view, I stop and sit down.

"Okay, let's get this out on the table, once and for all," I say looking up at him, as he hasn't sat yet.

"I told you, gyal, there's war coming …"

"Look," I huff, cutting him off. I'm frustrated. "*This* is what I've been told." I hold up my fingers as I fire back at him everything he *has* told me. "*One*. You married a woman who wasn't who you thought she was. *Two*. You lost her and your child. *Three*. You think I'm that missing child. *Four*…"

"I don't *think* I know anything; I *know* you are mine." Max cuts me off, narrowing his eyes at me, sitting down on the other rock with an angry grunt, his accent stronger now.

"And what *makes* you so sure Max?" I call him by his real name when we're alone. "Because we have the same colored eyes? We should have a DNA test, but that'd mean going into Las Vegas, and it could take months. If what you're saying about this war has any truth to it, then we don't have that kind of time." I run one hand over the top of my head in frustration, at the same time he does the exact same thing.

"You might have my eyes, gyal, but you look just like your mother," Max tugs a leather wallet, that looks like it's seen better days, out of his back pocket, pulls out a crumpled photo, and passes it to me. The photo appears to have been handled many times over.

As I scan it, I gasp.

Except for my short dark curly hair and my caramel-colored eyes, I could be sisters with the young woman in the photo.

The woman has long, dark chocolate hair hanging in a braid over one shoulder, and dark brown eyes, but other than that we look very similar.

She is more petite than me, with fuller breasts, and curves in all the right places, whereas I am tall, with smaller breasts and not so many curves. Our faces, however, are extremely similar. Same high cheekbones, almond-shaped eyes, full heart-shaped lips, and A-line nose. Even her smile appears to be the same as mine, or the other way around. Her clothes consist of a white peasant top which shows off her cleavage, and a long billowing skirt, again peasant style, paired with thin strapped flat sandals.

Next to her, with his arm possessively around her shoulders, holding her body close to his is a much younger Max. He isn't wearing a cut, only a white t-shirt, and cutoff jeans.

"Okay, so we look similar," I concede, my anger dissipating a little.

"So, so much likkle gyal." Max's voice softens, and his eyes hold a saddened look.

"I'll admit, you're beginning to sway me, but there's some questions I need to ask, and I need honest answers. If you *don't* answer me truthfully, I'm done." I look him straight in the eye as I declare this, so he'll know I'm serious.

"Okay, hit me," replies Max, straightening his shoulders as if preparing himself for a real punch.

I breathe out slowly, preparing myself for the answers I've wanted since we first started this dance.

"If S-Striker…" his name on my tongue causes my throat to tighten and it comes out with a croak, "knew who I was, why didn't he tell me? And why did he bring me to Nevada with him?" My shoulders tense as I watch for Max's reactions to my questions.

"That's one of the things I need to ask him, gyal, as soon as I see him. Where is he?" Max's voice sounds gruff.

I guess it's time for me to be honest too.

"He … he …" This is harder than I thought. "S-Striker is *dead*. Two years ago, now." I finally grate out stuttering over his name.

"*What*? *How*?" His scowl and thinned lips show he's concerned about this turn of events.

"Road accident. Must've been a leak in his gas tank, and a spark set it off. His truck exploded while he was out driving with …. No one survived." I'm trying to get the words out, but they feel thick and keep sticking in my throat. Usually Cricket or Harmony relate any events from that day. I haven't had to say it out loud before.

"Driving? Why wasn't he on his bike? Explosion?" Max looks at me confused, jumps up, places his hands on his hips and paces up and down in front of me for a minute or so. Huffing out a breath, he sits again before continuing, "Fuck! *Wait*, you said *no one*? Was there someone *else* in the truck?"

The tears I've been able to abstain from for some time now begin to sting my eyes. I'm going to have to say it.

I don't want to say it.

Closing my eyes tightly, I wait for the tears to fade.

I don't want to say it.

The thought is causing my freaking PTSD to kick up. My breath comes in gasps. The world begins to spin, and there are bees buzzing in my brain.

I stand from the rock I had been seated on and try to stumble away on unsteady legs.

I need to go.

Please, I beg silently, *don't ask me again.*

Max jumps to his feet also and leaning forward grasps my upper arms with his big hands turning me to face him.

"*Whoa*, gyal, *whoa*. You've gone white as a sheet. Who else was in his truck? *Tell* me." He demands, looking me straight in the eyes.

"If you are who you say you are, *your granddaughter*! My baby girl was in the truck with him." The words feel like sandpaper on my tongue. *I can't tell him they were going to buy me a surprise birthday present at the time of the accident.* "They *died*, Max!" I practically scream at him.

The last of my strength gives out and I crumble to my knees, the oxygen I need refusing to be drawn in. I don't get to gauge Max's reaction before the world goes black.

13
_____

THERE'S A FAMILIAR ODOR SURROUNDING ME, AND I can hear whisper yelling nearby. As the world comes back into focus, I open my eyes to see Nitro and Cricket having what looks like some *really* harsh words with Max.

Somehow, I'm in one of the motel rooms, lying in a hard queen size bed.

I hate motels.

The smell of them makes me nauseous.

Cricket is standing at the door to the room, between Max and the bed, holding Boris casually over her right shoulder.

"I'm sorry," grunts Max in a loud whisper, "But I need to speak with her as soon as she wakes up. I need to know…"

"*You* seem to be the reason she's laying here right now," my VP cuts him off gruffly, "and *we* need to know what happened. You're not getting anywhere near her until we're sure she's okay. So, *fuck off*, let us deal with the fallout of whatever happened, since you won't give us any details, and then *we'll* decide if she's safe with you or not." Cricket means business, and Nitro nods in agreement.

They always have my back.

I clear my throat which alerts them I've come to, and they push Max out the door, albeit with some effort, shut it, then return to my bedside.

Cricket sits on one side of the bed, Nitro on the other.

"Hey Jez, you gave us a scare. The only reason that asshole is still breathing right now is the fact that you are. Oh, as well as the fact we're outnumbered right now." I know Cricket is trying to lighten the mood a little, but I can see the worry lines around her mouth and eyes as she smiles, trying to reassure me. "When he came charging back here with you slung over his shoulder, I nearly lost it."

"Give us the word and we'll start kicking ass and taking names, Jez," Nitro chimes in, grasping my wrist and looking at her watch, as she checks my pulse.

"Maybe you best hold off on kicking ass for a minute or two," I say quietly as Nitro lets go of my wrist, and I pull myself up into a sitting position. "I need to tell you a few things first, but I need you to swear it goes no further. I know we don't keep secrets from our top people, but until there's absolute proof, I need this kept on the down low. No judgement okay?" I look pleadingly at both of them in turn, as they nod their heads in unison, agreeing. Taking a deep breath, then blowing it out slowly to settle my nerves, I tell them everything I've been told so far by Max, or Lucifer, as they know him, and everything *I've* told him, right up to my massive PTSD attack and subsequent blackout.

I am an MC president. I don't faint.

When I've finished relaying my story, leaving out very little, both women look at me wide eyed.

"Well shit, Jez, it seems you truly *might be* the daughter of the devil, huh?" Cricket says with such wonder in her voice Nitro and I break into laughter.

Later in the day, Cricket lets Max into the room, but he isn't alone. Ghost is with him. Perhaps he thought his prez might need backup. Max gives an almost imperceptible shake of his head as I look at him questioningly. For some unknown reason Max has not let his number two in on what went on. Does he not trust his vice president? Or does he not trust me?

I believe it's the latter.

"How you feelin', gyal?" Max inquires, as he brings a chair over to the right side of the bed, turns it so the back of the chair's facing me and sits on it, leaning his forearms on the high back and placing his chin on his arms.

"I'm fine, these two are being royal pains in my ass by not letting me out of bed until I've had what they consider *ample bed rest*." I do air quotes with my fingers as I say this.

My eyes are not on Max though. They are on the GMF who is standing next to my bed, his eyes roving over me with a look that suggests he might want to be in the bed with me.

Where did I get that from?

"You good?" Ghost asks softly, in his whiskey and smoke voice. His hair is pulled back from his face today, and as he's standing with his right side to me, I can see the scar on the side of his face is healing nicely, although it will always be visible.

It adds to his appeal though.

Makes him seem edgier, sexier.

WTF?

"I'm *fine*," It comes out harsher than I meant to, and his eyes get a now familiar cold light to them.

"*Great*." He huffs out sharply, abruptly turning on his heels, and walking out of the room.

Great, I've succeeded in pissing him off yet again.

"Can we talk? We need to discuss the happenin's of this morning if you're up to it?" Clearing his throat, Max breaks into my thoughts, and I realize I'm still staring at the doorway Ghost stormed out through.

I look up at my two bodyguards and they know I want privacy, so they head toward the exit.

Cricket stops before closing the door behind her, turns and looks at me, then at Max, and without taking her eyes off him states pointedly, her eyes narrowing, "If you need us, we're only next door, Jez. Boris is next to your bed."

With that the door closes and they're gone.

Max chuckles, "Very subtle that one." Then his face becomes serious as he adds, "It's good to know you have good people at your back. We're probably going to need them."

"They are, and they do. I've told them most of what you've told me, but I asked them not to repeat it until I give the word. We try not to keep secrets in our club. There was some trouble after the accident, which was my fault, but it's done now, and we try to be honest with each other. I don't want to involve the others until I know the full story." I don't think Max likes the way I say story, but to me it *is* a story, until I wholly and solely believe him.

"So … I had a grandbaby?" Max asks quietly, and when I look over at him, he is studying his hands contemplatively.

"Yes," I answer softly. "Her name was Marley."

There it is.

The first time I've uttered her name since her death.

"Was Striker …?"

"The father? *Hell no.*" I roll to my left side, bringing an extra pillow with me to hug like a security blanket as I relate how my baby girl came to be.

"I was attacked roughly five years ago. He was never caught. The police think it was someone from a rival gang wanting to teach me a lesson. They didn't like the fact Striker was encouraging a motorcycle club run by a woman, especially a Latino woman. I was cocky, and thought I was untouchable. Oh, how the harsh reality of life proved me wrong," I finish sarcastically.

Max sits unmoving while I tell him about going off alone one afternoon, into Las Vegas, looking for more recruits for my club, which I had done many times, despite warnings. Striker and Cricket had said on numerous occasions, they didn't think I should be going into the city alone, but I had ignored them. I like the solitude sometimes, just me, my bike, the road, and the desert. In Las Vegas I was anonymous and could do my research on candidates without any expectations. It made me vulnerable to other clubs looking to teach life lessons. This was also how I had found Nitro.

14

IN MONOTONE I NARRATE HOW MY BABY GIRL CAME to be.

"The *Yard House* restaurant plays great classic music and spectacular food. I was indulging in it when I overheard a woman on the next table talking on her phone. I leaned back in my chair, eavesdropping.

"Her accent was that of a New Yorker, if I was right, and she was vehemently telling whoever was on the other end of the line that she was done with them, whoever *they* were. She continued on, saying she had studied her ass off, and become the top of her class at whatever the job was, only to be knocked back time and time again for promotions because of her sex. Even though she was trying to keep her voice low, I heard her stating to the unknown caller that the only offers she had, included her sleeping with the controllers or handlers, and that was not going to happen, so they could shove the job up their tight asses. She was looking around for something better. I listened carefully the whole time she spoke. It was with a clipped, controlled voice, and though I could hear the anger dripping from her, she didn't become hysterical.

She must have hung up on them as the conversation stopped abruptly.

I sat in my chair contemplating what her something better might be.

The waitress caused me to jump as she unexpectedly appeared at my table.

"Excuse me, Ma'am, but the woman at the next table asked if it was okay if she joined you?"

I scrunched my lips up for a second, then shrugged. "Okay, that's fine."

Maybe she wanted to have a dig at me for eavesdropping. Maybe she was lonely. Hopefully, she wasn't gay, as that wasn't going to work for me.

Not having eyeballed the woman who had been speaking on the phone, I was surprised when a beautiful, slim, almost skinny, woman sat down in the seat next to me. Her ebony hair was in a tight bun on top of her head, and I judged her to be around twenty-five or six in age. Her eyes were dark chocolate, and her skin a creamy brown, and I could immediately see her Native American heritage. Her clothes were that of an office worker. She wore a gray pencil skirt, green blouse, and flat shoes.

"Hi, my name is Janet." She extended her hand to me, presumably to shake, which I did after a few seconds hesitation.

"I'm Jez," I gave her my name, dropping my hand from hers. "What can I do for you?"

"I know who you are. I've been hoping to track you down for a while, and then you walk right in here and sit at the table next to me. It's like karma or something." She gave me a wide-eyed innocent look.

"Why were you tracking me?" My eyes narrowed suspiciously even though she seemed to be open and honest with the fact she'd been trying to find me.

We had worked for several different groups but weren't high profile. That would interfere with our businesses.

Growling breaks into my reminiscing.

"What does Nitro have to do with you and my granddaughter?" Max is becoming a little impatient.

"If you want to know the full story, you have to be patient, old man." I glare over at him.

He sighs, waves his hand at me to go on, so I do.

"Janet explained to me that she'd studied most of her life to be in the … her job, but had quickly tired of the sexist, political bullshit and red tape that went on within it and had started to look for something else. With a love of motorcycles she'd gained from her brother, who was killed in the line of duty in Iraq, she began to wonder what it would be like if she quit her job, bought herself a bike and rode off into the sunset.

"After several months of research, she had hit upon our club, and decided she liked what she found and wondered if we would be a good fit. We weren't criminals, not that she could discover, but we didn't exactly seem to toe the line of the straight and narrow either.

"The thing that grabbed her though, was the fact the club had a woman president, and the diversity of the club members as well as loyalty to each other.

"After chatting for a few hours, and exchanging phone numbers, I left her at the restaurant and headed back to my hotel. I hadn't intended on staying the night but was intrigued by Janet enough that I was willing to stay and have one more meeting.

"I liked her honesty, and arranged a meet with her the following day, where I'd make my final decision whether to take her with me to meet the rest of my club or reject her as a prospective member.

"Cricket rang and I let her know I wouldn't be back that night.

"Not needing anything fancy, I found a small motel room off the strip, dumped my backpack in my room, left my bike out the front, and walked to a local bar for a drink.

"After I had a couple of tequila shots, followed by a beer, I headed back to my room, which was only a short walk. On the way my phone rang and when I answered I was surprised that it was Janet.

"She was a little worried that I was going to brush her off, but I assured her I was a woman of my word and that the meeting would go ahead irrespective of my decision. I also let her know where I was staying in case something came up and she needed to come to me."

That was a lucky move on my part.

"I had just hung up my phone, when my head began to spin, and by the time I made it to my room, I was staggering as though I was drunk.

"My room key dropped out of my hands several times

before I finally lodged it in the key hole and pushed the door open.

"As I entered the doorway to my room, I felt a presence behind me, but my reflexes were affected so badly I couldn't stop what happened next.

"A bag was shoved over my head and my legs were kicked out from underneath me. As my legs buckled, I felt my arms being pinned behind me.

"I remember hearing a man with a deep accent say, you are finally mine, *puta*. At the time I thought I'd heard his voice somewhere before.

"Everything was a blur, but I remember cable ties being placed around my wrists, then being held in a chokehold until everything went black."

"Fuck no. Tell me that bitch had not set you up!" spits Max, jumping to his feet, knocking the chair over, pulling me from my memories.

"She didn't. Do you think she'd be here if she did? Nitro turned out to be my savior. If it wasn't for her I might not even be here today." I watch Max calm himself and silently arch my eyebrows looking between him and the chair until he regains his seat, so I can continue.

Once he has righted the chair and is settled, I go on.

Closing my eyes, I hope not to let Max see the horror I feel at relaying that horrendous night, and quietly begin again.

"When I came to, the bag was still over my head, which was thumping; my hands and feet were tied at all four corners of the bed.

"I had been beaten and raped."

I neglect to mention the permanent reminders the animal who attacked me left behind, the ones that cannot be erased, including the metal screws in some of my bones holding them together.

"Whoever it was, did this several times during the night and into the morning. I don't know how many times he raped me, but not a word was spoken. We also think he kept drugging me. I remember trying to threaten him in the beginning, then I tried pleading, but that resulted in being beaten more.

"Falling in and out of unconsciousness, I had no idea how long I'd been subjected to what that sick fuck did to me. One time I thought I heard a knock on the door. I took the opportunity and screamed, well gurgled, as I had had no water or food, so my throat was dry, and when the knocking stopped, I thought whoever it had been mustn't have heard me.

"Screaming earned me a punch to my face which knocked me unconscious again.

"The next thing I knew there were police everywhere, and Janet was untying me, covering me with a blanket, and I was being loaded into an ambulance.

"I'd missed our meeting, and when I didn't answer my phone, Janet had come looking for me. When I didn't answer the door, she went to leave, thinking I was ditching her, when she noticed blood on the door frame. She heard me try to scream, and not knowing what was on the other side of the door, she called a cop friend of hers, and the rest is history."

I purposely leave out the fact that I'd been a virgin until that night.

Heaving a sigh, I'm surprised I feel lighter having all this off my chest.

What is more surprising is Max's face when I finally lift my eyes to look at him.

"So, what happened to the animal who raped and assaulted you?" The murderous tone in Max's voice even frightens *me*. "He had better be a dead mon," he growls.

"If he's not he will be," snarls an all too familiar voice, causing my eyes to widen in shock as I hadn't heard him enter the room.

Ghost is standing in the doorway, feet planted apart, arms crossed and an even angrier look on his face than Max has.

I hadn't heard him open the door; such is the pain of my memories.

"N-No. No, he's not." I stammer, "I don't even know what he looks like. He somehow got away between the knock on the door and the police arriving. He disappeared, and I was no help to the police. I was drugged and beaten unconscious for most of it. The doctors call it selective amnesia. There are triggers, like today for instance, that cause PTSD attacks. I don't usually talk about it; I try not to even think about it; that's how I control them." I hang my head, embarrassed.

Oh. My. God.

Not only have I told someone who could be my father every sordid detail, but his vice president now knows at least part of it.

I feel myself tearing up and swallow, biting my lower lip as I breathe deep, schooling my features, refusing to let them see my shame and humiliation.

After all, I've spent years perfecting this. I also refuse to acknowledge Ghost's presence, instead look Max in the eyes and say quietly, "So now you know how Marley came to be. You also know how she died. Now if you don't mind, I'd like some peace and quiet."

With that comment, I roll onto my other side, so my back is to Max, and close my eyes, pretending to sleep.

That is not going to happen.

My chest hurts, as my heart breaks all over again.

Once I hear the door close, and I scan the room to make sure I'm alone, I let the pain out, burying my face as I scream into the pillow with an agony so strong, I feel it in my entire body.

15

When I awake, it's dark. The smells of the dank musty room surround me, and for a second, I panic, stuck in a memory from the past.

My eyes pop open, and I pull my arms close to my body. It's then I realize I'm not tied down, and this is not the past.

The fear passes.

I roll off the bed and head in the direction of the bathroom.

As I exit, the bathroom light reflects off something as I flick the switch off, and I still my movement toward the bed, instantly hoping that Cricket has left Boris on the floor at the side of the bed where I'm currently standing.

My eyes adjust to my surroundings, and I realize what, or rather who, is in the room.

Reaching back, I flick the bathroom light back on.

Ghost is seated on the chair Max had been sitting on while I related my tale of woe to him.

"What are you doing here?" I challenge him.

"This is my room," he deadpans.

"Oh. Sorry to put you out. I'll go. Cricket and Nitro will have a space for me." Searching for my jeans in the dull light, I intend to slip into them, as I'm only wearing my underwear and tank top, but they must have been kicked under the bed and I scramble in vain.

"There's enough space in that bed for two. Everyone's asleep. It's three o'clock in the mornin'." Ghost stands and stretches. Removing his cut, he slings it on the back of the chair he was sitting on and reaches for his belt buckle. As he undoes the button of his jeans the light I had switched back on in the bathroom illuminates his six pack and outlines the V dipping down into his jeans. Even though my inner body seems to be doing a happy dance, I place my hands on my hips and narrow my eyes at him.

I am *not* having sex with him.

Ghost's eyes flick up to mine. "Not what I was thinking, I need sleep." *How did he know what I was thinking*? Or did I say that out loud?

Okay then.

I shuffle back into the bathroom and close the door, needing some deep breaths before I go back out there.

You can do this, Jez. It's just sleeping. I try to psyche myself up.

He obviously doesn't want to have sex with me.

Who would, you freak?

I understand, but for some reason, I still feel hurt.

———

When I re-enter the room, I stand for a few moments, watching the massive man who is now lying on his back, on the left side of the bed, on top of the covers, in only a pair of tight black boxers. He appears to be sound asleep, and I let my eyes wander appreciatively over his body. Ghost is perfection personified, even to someone who has not had much, okay *no*, experience, and I can feel my core warming, causing me to clench my legs together, my heart racing at the sight before me.

I tip-toe around to the other side of the bed and gently climb in, trying not to disturb him. Even though this is a queen bed he takes up a lot of space, so I roll to my right side to give him more room.

After all it *is* his bed.

Sometime during the early hours I begin to feel extremely hot. It takes a few seconds before I realize Ghost has rolled over, wrapped one massive arm around me pulling my back tight against his chest, and there's a large bulge wedged against the crack of my ass.

My mouth tastes like cotton.

I try to escape his grasp, but he holds me tighter.

It doesn't escape my notice that we fit together perfectly.

"Sleep Jez, I got you," is breathed quietly in my ear.

As if we aren't connected, my body instantly relaxes while my brain tells me to get up and run, but then my brain decides to agree, *without telling me*, with my body, and I fall asleep.

For the first time in a long time, I sleep soundly and dreamlessly.

When I wake again Ghost is gone.

Max and I agree next morning, to get his people packed up and head for our compound.

I need to find out the rest of the story between Max and his woman if I'm to believe them to be my mother and father, and only then, *if I am satisfied with the answers*, do I need to let the rest of my club know what's going on.

More importantly though, is that I need to be with my club, my family, helping to protect them if this war is really coming.

16

MAX AND HIS MEN TOOK MOUSE'S BODY OUT TO THE desert this morning to be buried. He has no family other than his brothers in the MC, and no woman, so no one will miss him except his brothers.

Nitro, Cricket, and I stay behind at the motel while they say their goodbyes.

There are a few women from the Satans Vultures club grouped by the motel reception doors.

It's a hot day, and the three of us are sitting on some old Adirondack chairs, under a covered area, near where a swimming pool used to exist in the rundown motel's glory days. We are fanning ourselves with pieces of cardboard, drinking cold bottled water, and chatting about the events of the past few days, when some of the other club's women approach us.

The spokeswoman, a tall leggy female with short spiked, bleach-blonde hair, is wearing denim barely-there shorts, and a pink tank top with no bra. Her ample fake tits are practically falling out of the top when the stripper heels on her feet come to a stop in front of us.

Really? Stripper heels in the damn desert?

She crosses her arms and taps her fake pink nails on her skin while scowling down at us. Her makeup is on too thick, as is her black mascara. The blood red lipstick doesn't suit her collagen-filled lips either.

The other women stand behind her.

She must be their fearless leader.

"So, you bitches think you're too good for us, huh? Sittin' over here fanning yourselves, waiting for *our* men to come back," She emphasizes the word 'our', as if she owns them. "Well you're *not* better than us, and you can keep away from them."

We three sit and stare back at them, our faces schooled, without replying. Blondie must think she has us scared, and gathering courage steps forward, coming to a stop in front of me. She leans down, and I catch a good look at her cleavage and the small bluebird tattoo above her right breast before raising my eyes to hers. She pokes her finger at my forehead.

"And as for *you*, *you* stay away from Ghost. He's *mine*," she states with confidence. "I saw you coming out of his room before, *slut*, and I'm warning you. If I see you so much as *look* at him again I'll rip your eyes out of that ugly black head of yours." She pokes me with her finger harder and harder as she threatens me.

Enough is enough.

My anger rises.

Okay, it doesn't rise, its boiling over.

We didn't ask them to come over here; we didn't give them any cause to behave like they are, and I won't stand for it a moment longer.

They need to know their place, and if Max hasn't taught them, I will.

I leap up out of my chair without warning, pushing it backward with the force as I do. Placing both hands behind Blondie's head, I pull her face down sharply onto my knee. Her nose snaps. I feel it as blood instantly sprays on my jeans.

Damn, that'll be hard to get out. I should've worn my leather pants, at least it would wipe off.

I sidestep her as she falls forward, grab the back of her tank top, stick my foot in her ass and push, letting go of her at the same time. Blondie flies forward, sprawling awkwardly face first on the hard ground.

"You broke by fuckid dose!" Blondie screeches as she scrambles up off the ground onto unsteady feet.

"You asked for it. Besides, it matches your lips now." I school my features, keeping my voice level so she doesn't realize how pissed I am that she referred to Ghost as *hers*.

I don't understand where this pang of jealousy is coming from.

Nitro grabs Blondie by the throat with one hand and her tank top with the other as she staggers upright, and lunges for me. Dropping to one knee, she sweeps the woman's legs, and proceeds to flip the bleeding woman onto her back on the ground. Blondie huffs as she hits the ground, yet again, as the wind is knocked from her lungs.

A couple of the other women begin to move forward in defense of their stupid friend, but when Cricket stands up, pulling Boris out from under her chair, they freeze mid step.

"Uh uh uh, I wouldn't if I were you," Cricket singsongs calmly, her nose twitching up and down like a rabbit and waggling her pointer finger at them. She extends her arms in front of her, both hands around Boris's handle and gives them a good look at her weapon. "That is unless you don't want your biker buddies to ever want to fuck you again. Cos if I hit you with Boris here, you're going to be a *hell* of a lot uglier than you are now."

"But she beat Sugar, we can't let her get away with that," whines one of the women at the back of the pack.

"*She*," Cricket points to me, emphasizing the words, "is *our* goddamned *president*. *She* can beat *who* the fuck she wants, *whenever* the fuck she wants." Moving the direction of her arm slightly so she is pointing at Blondie, Cricket continues, "That bitch started this, and she deserved what she got, and worse. So, take her and get the fuck out of our sight before we tell Lucifer to leave your asses here. You can be in our compound by tonight, safe and sound, or you can stay out here where whoever or whatever got Mouse can get you all too." She swings Boris menacingly over her shoulder as if she's going in to bat at a game, Cricket snaps "Now piss off, *all* of you."

One of the women, a short brunette, who I later find out is named Rosie, reaches for the blonde, helps her off the ground, and puts an arm around her waist to steady her. I have to give her points for loyalty.

Before they leave, the brunette looks at me with wide blue eyes, and says, seemingly with awe, "You're the *president* of your club? Wow. I ain't never heard of a female prez before. Wow." Then she leads the bleeding, winded Blondie away.

Max is pissed when he hears what happened while they were out burying their brother, and I hear him shouting at the women about how they need to mind their business and their manners when it comes to the Broken Halos MC, especially me.

He also tells them in no uncertain terms they better be on their best behavior, once we get to the BH's compound, or they'll find themselves stranded outside the gates with no men and no backup.

Everyone is packed up, and the bikes are readied for the road.

Those few women with property cuts climb on the backs of their men's rides, and I try to stifle a smirk when I see Blondie sidle up to Ghost, who is sitting on his black and chrome FLSTF Fat Boy, with ape hangers, and attempts to put her leg over his bike, only to be told, *I'm guessing at his gestures as I can't really hear what he says*, to get her ass on the back of Slimeball's ride.

Blondie stamps her foot in the dust like a petulant child and storms over to Slimeball and his bike. He, in turn scowls at Ghost, but moves forward enough for her to ride bitch.

I take note that Blondie aka Sugar isn't wearing a cut, which means she is no one's property.

For some reason I'm relieved.

Eventually Lucifer strolls to his ride, backs it out and starts it up, waiting for the rest of his club to get into formation.

I roll up next to Lucifer, and again I notice his VP is at the rear of the pack.

Ghost hasn't spoken a word to me about last night; in reality he hasn't spoken to me at all.

I'm a little annoyed about that.

Checking to make sure Cricket and Nitro are ready, I notice Nitro is riding next to Doc, who has a black bandana tied over his head, his hair's in a single braid, and he has a black bandana with a white skull mouth tied around his face.

He obviously doesn't wear a helmet.

The SV road captain gives the rollout signal, and he does so by raising his right arm with his pointer finger in the air, he rolls his hand in a circle, then dropping his arm slightly, points in the direction we are travelling.

The ground shakes with the rumbling bikes, and as it always does, I know my panties are wet. *Fuck, Harleys turn me on.* Max and I take off after the RC, and the rest follow.

17

TIME SEEMS TO PASS QUICKLY, AND WHEN WE FINALLY stop at the gates to the Broken Halos' compound, I use my phone app to punch in the code. The gates are electronic and open to allow us to ride into our compound in the same formation as we were riding in on the road.

Assuming everyone's inside, I press the button to close the gates again, and as they do I turn toward them, noticing Ghost isn't with us.

"Hey Lucifer, Ghost isn't here yet," I shout, referring to his road name in front of his men. He hasn't turned his bike off yet.

Switching his ride off, Max swings the stand out, then climbs off, dropping his black helmet on the seat.

"Shit. Where did he go? He was behind us all the way, I'm sure." Max has a worried scowl on his face, and he rakes his eyes over the rest of his club members as they each line their bikes up, turn off their motors, and disembark.

Patting himself down, Max appears to be looking for something.

He finally finds it in his shirt pocket, and pulls his cell phone free, hitting speed dial.

"Yo," he says with that deep man voice guys seem to use when they're on the phone. "Where the fuck are you?"

Obviously, Ghost is explaining something to him, and Max's scowl deepens.

"So, you didn't get them? Did you recognize anything about them?" He listens again, then hangs up.

Max stands still for a few moments, and I notice a nerve in his jaw ticking.

"*Fuck!*" he yells without warning, causing everyone to jump. His brothers are all looking at him nervously.

"What's going on" I ask quietly, "Tell me. Is Ghost alright? What happened? Did he get a flat? What?"

Max is looking at me oddly, like he's trying to work something out, then he schools his face, leans forward and whispers in my ear, "We had some trackers, so he fell back to try and figure out who they were, but they backed off and went in the other direction."

He then steps back and says loud enough for everyone to hear, "He had to take a piss. He'll be here in a minute. Take care of your rides, brothers. The old ladies and whores can see Jez and her people about where they'll be bedding down, and any chores they need to help with."

Blondie looks like she's about to say something, but the brunette grabs her by the arm and drags her toward the clubhouse.

Rooms have been assigned, married men with their old ladies in tow getting preference, while single men and whores are left to squabble over the spaces left.

Some of the bikes need tarpaulins erected around and over them, so if the wind picks up they won't be covered in the fine sand that gets into everything. There's not enough room in the barn for everyone's bikes, as all the BH's are in the compound tonight. The other club have only brought one cage with them.

The higher ranked in the Satans Vultures get top priority on the spaces left in the barn.

The SV's old ladies and whores have made themselves useful, *under Max's orders*, and are cooking up a storm in the kitchen. I heard Hope grumbling about how they better clean up their mess, because she wasn't going to do it for them, no matter what nice shit they cooked.

I told her to shut the fuck up and be grateful she and Luke didn't have to do all the cooking. Noticing Luke hanging out in the kitchen, eyeing off Blondie aka Sugar, I gave him some extra yard duties to dull his horny ass down. He doesn't need to get his ass whupped for touching another club's whore, *especially that one*.

I wonder what Ghost sees in her.

The thought makes me shiver.

The music and alcohol is flowing, and as I look around the room I see other SV's eyeing off some of my club members, and vice versa. I don't mind them intermingling if it's consensual.

However, when I notice Slimeball's eyes following Harmony's every move, I take offence for her.

It's time to lay down some rules.

Vaulting onto the bar, I place my fingers in my mouth and give a loud, shrill whistle. Automatically the music shuts down and all noises cease.

"Okay, listen up and listen good. You are in the Broken Halos MC compound by *my* invitation. For those who don't know who I am let me introduce myself. I am not an old lady nor am I a sweetbutt. I am Jezebel, president of the Broken Halos MC and I make the rules. So listen closely cos I'm not gonna repeat myself." Murmuring among some of the other club members starts up at that statement. "Yes. You heard correctly. I am the *president* of the Broken Halos MC. If you don't abide by my rules you will be dealt with accordingly. You got that? This is my club, my compound, my rules. The rules of the Broken Halos MC include the following. You break it, you pay for it. No one causes unnecessary friction. Oh, and you fuck it, it better be consensual. You get me?"

There are a few grumbles and whispers, and I see Slimeball's lips screw up in a sneer, so I make sure they all got the message.

Placing a hand behind one ear I yell, "I can't hear you."

There's a resounding "Yes, Prez" from the crowd.

The music starts back up as soon as I jump down from the bar and everyone resumes where they left off before I interrupted them.

It's well after ten pm before Ghost makes an appearance,

one of my club members having let him in the gate on his arrival.

Even though I'm on the opposite side of the room, I feel his presence as soon as he enters.

He's wearing his hair down, and no shirt, only his cut, so I can see every defined muscle from his broad chest to his six pack and narrow waist. Low slung, faded denim jeans cling to his legs, stretching tight at his crotch. Black biker boots with spiked studs on the toes are on his feet. His huge biceps look thicker than my thighs. Both his arms have tattoos from the elbows up, and he has leather cuffs on his wrists, like when I first saw him, but these are brown leather with pointed silver studs on them. Other than the hint of tattoos at his neck, his chest is bare of everything, except some minimal hair, and that fine blond line dipping down from his navel to the top of his low slung jeans. The scar on his face is still a little red at the edges.

Ghost stops when he reaches me, leaning forward slightly, like he wants to whisper something in my ear. He smells like leather and spice.

"I got something you want?" is breathed in my ear as he leans over me.

Shit.

Was I staring at him the whole time he walked toward me?

With that voice and his breath in my ear, I can feel myself getting wet, and he hasn't even touched me.

No ... no ... no. Stop right there.

I curl my hands into fists, fighting the urge to place them on his muscled chest, and coolly raise my eyes to meet his.

"Not that I can think of," I deadpan. "I see you still can't find a shirt."

Then, me being me, I have to go and spoil it all by babbling "Maybe you should go see your old lady-to-be and have her find you one."

Ghost immediately straightens his body, his eyes turn to ice, and he's now openly scowling at me.

"I don't have a fuckin' old lady, and don't ever intend to," he growls in that sexy pissed off smoke and whiskey voice of his.

I know I should apologize, and open my mouth to do so, but I don't get the chance as he brushes past me and storms out the back door, letting it slam behind him.

Okay, I did it again. Seems no matter what I say he gets pissed at me.

Alright, I know I deliberately poked at him. What can I say?

It pisses me off that someone besides me might have been worried about him when he didn't arrive with the rest of us. It also pisses me off I *was* worried about him.

The night wears on, the Satans Vultures women feed everyone, and I must admit it's a great feast.

I have been formally introduced to all six of the SV women now.

Blondie aka Sugar is a club whore. She knows what she is, but thinks she has a chance of becoming Ghost's old lady. Obviously, he hasn't told her he never intends to have one.

Rosie is the little brunette who picked Sugar's ass up off the ground when she got her beat down. She's not pretty in the sense of the word, but she's not ugly either. At about five foot two in height, she's a curvy young brunette with hazel eyes, a button nose and thin lips. I'd guess her to be around twenty-one years of age. Rosie's road name arises from the fact that when she orgasms, her cheeks go rosy red.

Several of Max's men filled me in on that little fact.

As if I needed to know.

Cheetah *is* an old lady, but I'm not up to speed yet on her man's name. At around five feet seven, she is tall and sleek. Her hair is golden brown and cut in a bob. If you met her on the street, you would probably think she's a businessperson of some type, not an old lady to a dude in a biker club. She has hazel colored eyes, an A-line nose, and full lips. Apparently, her name came from the fact that she kept trying to run away from her now husband, who is a meek looking man, *for a biker.*

Shameless has long, flaming red hair, stands at around five feet four and has modeliscious beauty. She has a sweet smile, and her doll like green eyes light up every time her new husband is near her. Her road name tells it all. She will fuck her husband anywhere, anytime, in front of anyone. They've already been at it on the pool table while everyone roared encouragement.

Butter is a curvy Latina with long dark hair, chocolate eyes and smooth, silky tanned skin and a white toothy smile. Apparently aptly named because butter is easily spread, and so is she.

Then there's Baby. She sounds like she's on helium when she speaks, and if I had to listen to her day in, day out, I think I would strangle her. She pouts and gets upset when she doesn't get her way, but with the huge pouty lips she has, I can guess why they keep her as a club whore. She also has huge blue *deer in the headlight* eyes that make her constantly look surprised. Baby is about five feet two, curvy, with big tits and a round ass that I bet the men just *love*. Not that I'm jealous.

18

LOOKING UP FROM MY SEAT ON AN OLD COMFY BLACK leather lounge chair, that has Cricket sitting on one arm of it, and Tinker on the other, shooting the breeze with me, I see Max and Ghost having what looks like an extremely heated discussion near the back door. Tinker asks me something, distracting me for a moment, and when I look back up, both men are gone, and the back door is just closing.

Excusing myself from the conversation, I get to my feet and casually wander to the outside deck, curious to see what's going on between the two. For a president and vice president, these two men don't appear to be seeing eye to eye. I think to myself maybe that's how other clubs do things, making me glad that mine doesn't.

We have a democracy here, and the majority vote wins, unless I *totally* don't agree with it. That's the way we roll.

I watch as they wander over to the barn where the bikes are kept, and as if a sixth sense warns me, I stick to the shadows, following them.

They wouldn't know there's a small entry at the right side of the building, which was probably designed for an animal at the time the barn was built, so I slip around the side and in through the door.

Following the murmur of voices, I ease my way around the packed shed toward them.

"You can't fuckin' tell her the whole truth, old man. She may be an innocent in all this, but if you want to get that sonofabitch, you need to stay on track. She'll be protected, you have my word," Ghost is saying.

I can barely make out their silhouettes in the darkness.

"She's my daughter, Ghost. I don't have definite proof, but I feel it in *here*." I hear a thud like Max is thumping his chest.

"We'll have confirmation of that soon. I took samples while she was at the motel and delivered them to the appropriate people. They'll have an answer for us sooner than anyone else could. You took an oath, that if they got you out, you would get them within reaching distance of Hernandez, maybe even Sanchez. She may be the only way to do that. If she knows what's going down, she may let it slip to the wrong people, and we'll lose our chance." My eyes are becoming accustomed to the dark, and I see Ghost's silhouette reach up and run his fingers through his hair, which I have picked up on as being an unconscious movement when he's frustrated.

Ghost's voice is softer as he says, "Look, I understand your need to protect her, Luc, but if you want to stay a free man, we have to play by *their* rules. We cannot deviate from the plan. They already have a fix on where we are, fuck knows how. There may be a mole in our ranks, or maybe in hers. I don't understand how they've got this close, this soon." He huffs a sigh. "I thought we would have more time. If there is a rat, and you let her know the full reason why we're here, you could be letting yourself in for a whole lot of hurt. We know she's a recovering junkie. Are you sure she's completely clean? If she isn't, we may be back to square one."

"I'm sure she's clean. You've seen her, does she look like she's a junkie? My Jez is a good girl, I know it. If we could tell her the real reason we're here I know she'd cooperate." Max's voice sounds hoarse.

Questions are running through my head.

How do they know?

After Marley died along with Striker on that fateful day, when they went to Las Vegas to buy me a birthday present, I fell into a stupor, drinking anything I could lay my hands on, and taking any pill I could find, or buy, to dull the pain of my loss. My baby girl may have been conceived by evil, but she was my angel, and I couldn't see the way ahead without her in my life. It was only when I accidentally overdosed, Cricket and some of my club members stepped in, deciding on some tough love, and day by painful day helped me extricate myself from my dependence. They made me realize there was a whole family, my MC, that was hurting too, and they needed me as much as I needed them. That's when I offered up my President's chair and was unanimously voted into keeping it. The whole of the Broken Halos MC showed me they cared for me not just as their president, but as a person, so I remained in my position, and fought the darkness.

I still do.

I thought they didn't know about me until Striker told Max.

What did Ghost mean by *they got you out*?

Had Max been locked up? In prison? For what?

I step back, deep in thought and accidentally knock something in the darkness, causing it to slide to the ground.

'*Fuck*. Who's there?" I hear Ghost grunt as he stumbles in the dark toward where I am standing.

Squatting down on my haunches, I quietly make my way to the small door and on escaping to the outside of the building, run full tilt around the side of the barn, and head to the back of the compound. I don't stop until I reach the two headstones.

I half fall, half sit on the ground in front of them, listening for footsteps.

Then, realizing where I am, I do something I haven't been able to do until tonight.

I reach out and touch my baby girl's headstone with a shaking hand. The moon is full, and I can just make out the writing on it.

MARLEY ANGEL CHAVEZ
AGE TWO
LOVED BY ALL
FLY FREE ANGEL

We didn't put her birthdate on the marble headstone, as I didn't think there was any point.

The other headstone is for Striker. Not knowing his full name, or birthdate, we couldn't put much information on it.

It reads.

STRIKER

PRESIDENT: SATANS VULTURES Nev Chapter

GIVE THEM HELL BROTHER

Neither of their bodies are buried here. There wasn't enough left of them after the crash and fire, and the authorities wouldn't allow it. Both were cremated, and their ashes scattered to the wind, except for the tiny piece of my baby girl in the vial around my neck.

Strangely, I find myself calming down quickly, sitting here under the moon, one hand on my angel's headstone, the other absently stroking the glass vial.

I hadn't been able to bring myself here before, as I thought I would lose it again, and I didn't think I could come back from that.

"I'm here now, baby," I whisper to the cold stone.

My thoughts go back to what I overheard in the barn tonight, and I'm trying to piece together the conversation, when I feel the hair on the back of my neck rise.

Coiled ready to strike, I hear Ghost growl, "Lucifer was worried about you."

Rising to my feet, I'm surprised to find he's quite close to me, and yet I hadn't heard a thing.

"Yeah, why?" I reply a little sharply. Whether it's because he's been able to get so close to me, or because my trust in him is waning after what I overheard, I don't know.

"Yeah, well he sent me looking for you," he growls, pissed off again. "What's this?"

He kneels on one knee, gazing at the headstones, probably trying to read them.

"Was Striker your old man?" he looks back at me over his shoulder.

"That's none of your business, but no, he wasn't. He came to my Grammy's house a few weeks before she died, then came back after she did and brought me here with him." I neglect to tell him Grammy died in a house fire while I was at school. Before she did, she told me if anything happened to her, or if Striker came for me I was to go with him, no questions asked.

I don't even know why I'm giving him *this* information. He has no right to know.

Then again, he probably already *does* know, so why did he bother asking?

"So, you never had an old man while you were with his club?" His voice sounds softer now, and the expression on his face, even in the moonlight looks ... *confused*?

"Nope." I pop the p, then hold my breath waiting for the next question.

"Hmm. Whose kid was she?" He changes the subject so fast, I don't have time to think.

"She was mine." I blurt without thinking.

Whoosh, the pain in my stomach and chest knock the wind out of me, and I gasp for air.

"Shit, sorry, are you okay? You don't have to talk about it if you don't want, but if you didn't have an old man, how did you have a kid? Or were you a ..." He sounds concerned as well as confused now, and I can see the crease between his brows get heavier as he frowns at me.

"The bastard ... who drugged and ... raped me may have been her father, but ...she was an innocent baby. It wasn't ... hers or my choice for her to be ... to be ... conceived like that, but she was my light and my life."

The words escape my mouth like sandpaper on a broken fingernail. My words are coming in gasps, as I desperately search for air, and tears blur my eyes, but for some unknown reason I need him to know that even though she was born as the result of violence, she was loved.

"I went off the rails after the accident. If it hadn't been for these people who surround me with uncondi-tional love and no judgement," I point toward the house, "I would have probably died with the weight of the grief I feel. They hold me together still on my darkest days, and build me back up, bit by bit." My voice is shaking now, as I try to hold it together. "This is the first time I've been here since these stones were laid. I didn't think I could ever do it, but I'm glad I came."

Ghost stands to his full height, grasping my forearms and pulling me gently with him. I stumble into his arms and he folds them around me, hugging me close.

My cheek is against his chest, and I can hear his heartbeat in my ear.

His scent reaches my nostrils, leather and earthy, and I feel a fluttering memory stir in the back of my mind like autumn leaves in the breeze, causing me to instantly relax, as a feeling of being safe overcomes me.

"I'm glad you made it back," he mumbles, and I could almost swear he means it.

I tilt my head back a little, looking up at him in the

moonlight, trying to pull back the fleeting memory, when as if in slow motion, he runs his right hand up my back, cupping the back of my head, he lowers his face to mine and kisses me. Not a hard, passionate kiss. He presses his lips to mine and holds them there. I gasp a little, maybe in shock, and he takes that opportunity to push his tongue into my mouth in a soft sensual way.

Without thinking, I respond in kind.

Oh. My.

"Hey Jez, you out here?" I hear Lordy calling me.

I disconnect our mouths and placing both hands on Ghost's chest, push him away.

He lets go and steps back, looking as surprised as me by what we'd been doing.

I turn on my heel and practically run toward where I think Lordy had called me from, without a backward glance.

"I'm here, Lordy. What's up?" I ask a little breathlessly.

"I think I need to ask you that question," Lordy smirks at me, looking toward the back door which Ghost is walking through.

He lets the door slam behind him.

"Piss off, I was out here enjoying the scenery," I lie. "What did you want me for?"

"Luke has to go into Las Vegas. Family shit. So, Tinker will be doing the rounds tonight; Cricket asked me to let you know."

Then he adds quietly, "He's a good-looking fucker; I'll give him that. If he batted for my side and I wasn't married, I would definitely climb that tree."

Lordy doesn't flaunt the fact he is gay, so when he says this kind of thing I take note.

"Nothing happened," I insist.

"You keep telling yourself that, Jez." His nose wrinkles up in amusement. "You might believe it, but I sure don't. Go look at yourself in the mirror." Lordy chuckles as he struts away.

I climb up the back stairwell to the second floor, and once inside quickly walk to the bathroom off my bedroom. Switching the light on, I move to the mirror to see what Lordy had meant.

My face is flushed, and my lips swollen from the kiss I'd recently partaken in.

I brush my lips lightly with my fingertips, remembering his on mine. I can still taste him.

Thank God I hadn't walked back into the clubhouse afterward. Everyone would have been asking me questions I didn't want to answer.

What was I thinking?

Obviously, I wasn't.

I shake my head in disgust.

Not five minutes before I let that giant motherfucker kiss me, he was discussing my life with my father, *if that's what he is*, like he knew everything about me.

I wash my face and brush my teeth, to rid myself of his taste, and once I feel some sort of normality, I wander back downstairs.

As I reach the bottom step, like a magnet, my eyes are drawn to Ghost, who is heading toward the back door with none other than Blondie walking ahead of him. She looks over her shoulder like she's seeking someone, and when her eyes find me, she smirks. Then she turns to

Ghost, places both hands around his neck, and pulls him in for a kiss, which he seems to evade and her lips land on his cheek instead. He leans down and whispers something in her ear, and she lets out a fake laugh as if he said something hilarious. Lowering her arms, she clasps her fingers in his large ones, as she pulls him out the door into the darkness.

I want to vomit.

19

THE NOISE DOWNSTAIRS GRADUALLY QUIETENS AS everyone grows weary or horny and wanders off to bed. As usual, I don't sleep much. Anger, confusion, and betrayal churn in my head like a freight train without brakes.

What did they mean by there was a plan?

When had he gotten my DNA?

I sit upright in bed with a gasp. That fucker must have gotten it while I was passed out.

No. that can't be right, Cricket and Nitro were with me.

Oh shit!

My hand clasps over my mouth as I realize the answer.

He did it while we slept in that damn bed together.

I sleep with my mouth open my Grammy used to tell me, so all he'd have to do would be swab the inside of my cheek with one of the cotton buds from the bathroom and put it in a plastic bag. That's why I had the strange taste in my mouth when I woke up.

Those TV shows like CSI show how they do it.

Motherfucker.

Balling my hands into fists, my anger is such that I want to go downstairs, *or next door*, tear Blondie off his huge cock and rip it off his big sexy body.

I truly am a sucker.

He played me well this time, but it isn't happening again.

Fool me once, shame on you, fool me twice, you will wish you had died.

I know that's not how the saying goes, but that's how *my* saying goes.

Knowing I'm not going to sleep any time soon, I scoot out of bed and find my phone, earplugs, some boy-leg panties, and a sports bra. Once dressed, I head to the gym to work out some of my aggression. Bypassing the weight and running machines, I head straight for the dance pole in the far corner of the room.

I do my warm up routine for about five minutes, stretching and loosening my muscles so I don't damage myself.

Strapping my phone to my arm, I choose Taylor Swift's songs, then placing my earbuds in, I climb the dance pole. Taylor Swift may be a girly girl, but I like her music, especially this album. The music is a little dark and dirty for her, and I wonder what caused her shift from the light and airy stuff she used to do. Perhaps someone hurt her, too.

The beat of *Look What You Made Me Do* begins and it's exactly what I need to work through my feelings, and hopefully tire myself out enough to get a few hours of sleep.

Once I'm at the top of the pole, I let the beat of the

music take over my body and wrapping one leg around the pole I lay my body horizontally against the cold steel, upside down, holding for ten seconds. Then I slowly pull myself up with my right leg, so my torso is vertical and lay my left leg against the pole, in a type of split. I hold each of these positions for ten seconds as it helps strengthen my core.

Switching positions, I grab the pole with both hands, a few inches apart, and let go of it with my legs. I then place my legs together, first bringing them up to my chest, bending my knees, on the right side of the pole, holding for ten seconds, then straighten out and bring them up in the same position on the left side of the pole, holding again for ten seconds, like a side tuck in gymnastics. I then position my legs, bend at the waist straight out either side of the pole and twist myself so I swing a full rotation around it.

While I'm rotating, with my crotch against the pole, I use the momentum to change my hand position, tuck my legs in and twist so that my back is now to the pole. Then, twisting my arms, and ducking my head through, I push my legs up to wrap around the pole, so I'm again upside down, and I let go with my hands. Holding this position for a few seconds, I then grip the pole with my left hand, and place both feet against the pole, rotate in a circular motion around it, as I slowly slide toward the floor.

I'm sweating profusely.

It's a great workout.

As I wipe the sweat off my neck and face I see movement in my peripheral vision and instinctively ducking low, I twist and punch at the intruder I know is behind me.

"*Jeeeus* H!" Dingo exclaims as I punch him in the balls, "*Fark ... Fark ... Ohhhh faaark*" as he falls to the floor, holding his crotch and getting paler by the second.

I cross my arms over my chest, not the least bit bothered by the fact that I'm only wearing underwear.

"What were you doing sneaking up behind me?" I huff indignantly.

"I wasn't bloody well sneakin' up on yuh, I was askin' yuh if yuh minded me runnin' in here on the machine while yuh did yuh pole thingy and yuh weren't answerin' me. Then I realized yuh had them ear plug thingamajigs in, so I stood 'n watched yuh routine. Yuh happened ta land in front of me. Oh faaark." Dingo then proceeds to dry reach from the pain of the hit to his lower regions.

I wince a little.

It had been a heavy hit, just as I'd been taught.

Don't ever pull a punch, no matter what, had been drummed into me from the start of my training. Feeling sorry for the poor guy now, I reach down and offer him my hand, but he skitters backward like he thinks I'm going to hit him again.

The stench of vomit is closeting the room, and I need to leave.

"I'm not going to hurt you ..." I huff, but he cuts me off.

"Huh," Dingo whines. "Yuh already did the damage. My poor dick is gunna turn black 'n drop off. I'll never get to procreate eva a fuckin' gen."

Damn he talks weird.

"Oh, stop your whining, I'm sure you can find someone to suck it better. Meantime let me get you up and get a bag of frozen peas to help with any swelling. If you're that worried, Nitro might take a look. She'll know if there's any permanent damage or not." I reach under his arm, and this time Dingo allows me to help him up, albeit groaning the whole time.

Bloody big baby.

We leave the gym, Dingo hobbling along still holding his nuts with one hand, his other arm around my shoulder. Supporting him, we walk slowly down the stairs and into the kitchen.

I sit him on a stool and turn to the fridge to look for a bag of frozen peas.

"Do yuh think Harmony would take a look at it instead of Nitro? I don't think I'd feel as embarrassed if she was lookin' at it." Dingo asks hoarsely.

I must've really hurt him, he isn't putting this on.

"I think Harmony's asleep. Most of the club is, so undo your pants and give me a look." I tell him as I turn from the freezer with the frozen bag in my right hand.

Dingo stands up gingerly, reaching for his belt buckle.

"The first offa I've got for a sheila to look at me dick in weeks and it's not even for sex," he grumbles as he drops his pants.

Standing at the edge of the kitchen counter, Dingo is hanging on to the end of it with his left hand so tightly his knuckles are white. His right thumb is hooked in his black boxers, and his faded blue jeans are now dangling around his kneecaps.

I stand between him and the refrigerator, holding the peas, which I've now wrapped in a dish towel to ease the shock when he puts them on his balls.

Handing the frozen bag off to him, I chuckle, albeit a little nervously, "Okay, sooky lala, give me a fucking look at your ballbag."

I am mortified to have to be doing this, but, well, I *did* hurt him, so I better see how badly. Kneeling down before him, I look up to gain permission to lower his boxers, and looking down at me, Dingo nods.

Grimacing as if I'm about to hurt him again, Dingo then closes his eyes and throws his head back with a sigh.

I peel the boxers down carefully, and his cock springs free. It isn't huge, *I don't think*, but big enough, and thick. The shaft's an angry purple color, and I'm unsure if that's from my punch, or if it always looks that way. It's also becoming fully erect. The blondish pubic hairs are abundant, and the area has a musky smell to it.

I try to ignore the rush of color to my cheeks. Dingo doesn't need to know how naïve I am when it comes to men's genitalia. "I'm going to have to handle it to see if there's any bruising, is that okay?" I ask softly, not wanting him to look down and get the wrong idea, as I kneel on both knees to keep me steady.

This is weird, handling a man's junk, especially a man I don't even know.

Dingo's voice is a little husky as he answers me, "Uh, yeah, okay."

I pull my phone from my pocket and turn on the torch app, so I can study his cock and scrotum closely. Lifting his balls as gently as I can, Dingo groans, and I don't think it's from lust. The torchlight shows I've bruised him severely, and there's a little swelling.

I'm beginning to feel *very* bad.

"Hand me the bag of peas, Dingo," I sigh, reaching up with my right hand, as he lowers them into my hand.

"How do they look?" he asks, with his eyes still scrunched up. "Sorry about … that … but it's been a while, so Liddle Ding is a bit excited to be handled, even if it is to be checked to see if he'll drop off tomorra." Dingo points at his erection without looking at me. "At least we know I can still get a boner. That's a good sign, yeah?"

Liddle Ding? Men name their cocks?

I try not to giggle at that.

"I don't think he's going to drop off any time soon, Dingo, but the boys will be horrifically sore for a while. There's a lot of bruising, and one of your nuts is starting to swell, so if I were you, I would take these peas to bed with you and keep them on the swelling as long as possible. Tomorrow morning I'll send Nitro to take a look …"

Dingo cuts me off, "Nah, Doc can check 'em out. No need for any more embarrassment than I'm already feelin'."

I raise the frozen bag to his scrotum, and Dingo hisses, "*Fark*, that's cold," he quips, jerking his body, which causes me to lose my balance. Reflexively I grab for the first thing that is available to steady myself, which happens to be Dingo's cock. "Fark, your hand's fucking cold woman," he yelps and jerks his body again. This movement causes the bag to dislodge from not only his nut-bag, but my hand as well and it hits me in the mouth before it falls to the floor...

"What in the fuck is going on in here?"

I instantly recognize Ghost's sexy growl and grasping onto the counter with one hand I rise to my feet, wiping at my mouth, as Dingo steps back from the end of the counter, his cock now flailing around, his boxers and jeans still down around his knees.

"Phhht, that was disgusting," I keep wiping at my mouth.

That bag had been on Dingo's nuts.

Yuck.

Snatching both boxers and jeans with one hand, Dingo pulls everything up in one go, affords me a glare, squats down to pick up his frozen bag of peas and flees the kitchen, knocking his shoulder against Ghost as he leaves.

The big mofo's body doesn't even budge.

His ice blue eyes lock onto mine.

"I asked what the *fuck* is going on?" he repeats, his voice as sharp as the razor edge of a fileting knife.

"Well, what do *you* think is going on?" I huff, shrugging one shoulder. I don't know why I don't tell him the truth, but the way he's looking at me, and speaking to me, pisses me off, hard core.

Do I detect a tone of jealousy in his voice?

"Why the fuck were you giving him head in the kitchen? Don't you have any morals?" he snarls at me.

What the … Oh no, he didn't!

"Listen here, *giant motherfucker*," I snap, revving myself up, but keeping my voice level. "I will *give head*, and I will screw *anyone*, *anywhere* I want. This is *my* fucking clubhouse, and *you* and everyone *else* in your pissy club can go *fuck* themselves, if they think I'm going to bow down to you. This is *my* club, this is *my* house, and I will not be questioned by *you*, or anyone else. *Do you understand me?*" As I let my temper take over I stomp over to where Ghost stands in the kitchen doorway, and to make my point I poke him in the chest, punctuating my words to show him how pissed off I am. "You have *no right* to be so indignant, when earlier *you* took Blondie out the back for a quick fuck. So, jam your sexual inequality bullshit … *Up. Your. Ass.*"

With that last exclamation, I storm past Ghost, heading to my room. Already embarrassed at being caught in what must have looked like an extremely compromising position, I'm more pissed that he thought he could do what he did earlier that night, after kissing me at the headstones, and then get angry at me when he thought I was doing the same.

Ghost catches my wrist as I pass by, and I stop. My breath stalls as I look up to see the stormy blue swirling in his eyes.

Why does he look like he wants to pin my body up against the wall and take me right there?

And why am I hoping he will?

Slowly I allow my eyes to graze over the rest of his body.

Blond streaked hair hangs down either side of his face. His beard and moustache have been recently clipped. His chest is bare, and he wears only his black jeans that hug his ass and legs just right. His feet are bare.

Damn those sexy feet.

As my eyes trail back up I notice his erection pushing hard against his tight jeans.

That must be painful.

Is that for me I wonder, then I ask myself if it might be because he got off on watching what he thought Dingo and I were doing, and that makes me want to vomit.

When my eyes reach his again I say quietly, "Let me go."

He does. I slowly step back through the kitchen doorway, holding his gaze, then when I'm nearly through it, I point to his bulging crotch.

My eyes flick up to see him run his tongue along his lower lip, then back down to the prominent bulge.

There's an invisible electric current running straight to my core and I feel my abdomen involuntarily clench.

Huh?

"You better go get Blondie to take care of that. She doesn't seem to have done a very good job first time around." Spinning on my heel as I finish what I have to say, I leave him standing in the kitchen.

I hear him curse as I trot up the stairs and head back to my room.

Ensuring both the bathroom door and my bedroom door are locked, I suddenly realize that I'm still in my underwear from my workout.

No wonder he thought Dingo and I were … *shit*!

20

THE NEXT MORNING AS I ROLL OUT OF BED, I CAN FEEL my muscles groaning at the mere thought of movement. Maybe I overdid the pole a bit last night, but at least I've had some sleep from the exercise. It might be a good idea to do it more often, to get those endorphins working.

Gathering those most loyal to the club in the meeting room this morning, I decide it's time to tell them what I know.

Nitro, Cricket, Lordy, Tinker, Shadow, Harmony, and a couple of other trusted members sit around the table chatting but quieten as I enter. They know something strange is happening, that there's a reason behind there being another biker club being invited to share our compound, and they're eager to find out the reason.

Luke and Hope are only prospects, so are not privy to this meeting, and others who have yet to prove their loyalty beyond a shadow of a doubt, have also not been invited.

Lucifer sits on one side of me, and Ghost sits across from us, glaring at me.

Obviously, Blondie must have been too busy last night to take care of him.

Back to business.

I call everyone to order, and Lucifer begins to relate the story so far.

He confirmed to me this morning my DNA had been taken without my knowledge, and the results came back, *sped up through a contact Ghost had*, that I *am* his daughter.

The news has not fully sunk in yet; I truly do have a father.

Since the death of Mouse, and the DNA confirmation, Max has decided all trusted personnel need to know what has happened in the past, albeit leaving out what he feels are minor details, and what's coming at us in the future. This way we can decide how to deal with it.

If they want to stay at my side, then they're more than welcome, but if they can't for some reason, deal with the supposed oncoming war, then I understand if they wish to leave. There's a knock on the door, and Hope enters with pots of hot coffee, cream, sugar, and mugs.

"I thought you could all use this," she says sweetly, with her heavy accent. "You cannot start the day without help."

I thank her and wait until she leaves before we start.

Max clears his throat and begins.

"None of you know me and my club, and I know you have all been wondering what is happening. I want you to listen to what I tell you without interruption. You can ask me questions, but not until I've finished. Why *I* am telling you and not your president, is because even *she* does not know the whole story yet."

He looks across at me, and I meet his gaze with curiosity, my brow creasing.

With a heavy sigh, he looks away, running his gaze over the others in the room.

Placing his hand on my shoulder, he gives a light squeeze, and I don't know if it's because he's nervous, or because he thinks I am.

"This girl ... no sorry ... this woman, is my daughter." Max pronounces woman *woomon*. There's a collective gasp from virtually all at the table, and Harmony's eyes are wide, her mouth in an 'O'. Cricket and Nitro know after I gave them the heads up while were in Nothing. Lordy's eyes narrow with suspicion.

Max continues, "Her mother and I lost her when my wife was kidnapped while in the middle of childbirth. While my wife lay dying as a result of complications, someone who had posed as her friend to get close to her, stole our likkle gyal away. This woman was supposed to give our baby to a very important person, my wife's father, but for some unknown reason she didn't, she kept her and ran. After a few weeks she gave our gyal to another woman, who as it turns out, had been one of my late wife's nannies until her and her family migrated to America. My wife died, and I had no idea where my likkle gyal was for a long, long time, until my friend Striker found her. He didn't tell me straight away." I look up as I notice his voice change, and Max has a confused look on his face. He sighs and shakes his head as he continues, "I don't know why he did not tell me straight away." Max looks at the ground as he repeats the sentence quietly. Then, taking a deep breath, continues. "He didn't tell me until long after my child's Grammy, as she called her, was murdered and her body left to burn in a fire, and he had brought her here to Nevada."

"*Murdered*?" I ask, my eyebrows shoot up in surprise, and my eyes widen. "They said it was an accident. They said a candle set the curtains on fire. Grammy fell asleep." I gasp this out exactly as it had been told to me by the police.

"I wish it had been, but it was no accident chil'." Max looks down at me with sadness etched in his eyes. "*They* had found you. If you hadn't been at school at the time of the fire, they would have taken you. Thankfully, Striker had already been in contact with your Grammy, and explained the situation to her. She was not surprised to find out that you were my Elida's daughter. Her and Striker had already spoken about what should happen if you were found."

"But I only saw Striker twice before Grammy ... died, and the third time was when he came and convinced me to come here with him," I mumble, looking at the table top, still shocked at the revelation that Grammy was murdered.

Because of me.

"He was watching over you day and night, likkle gyal, because he knew I couldn't." Max reaches down and grasps my chin lightly, lifting my face gently so my eyes raise up, levelling with his caramel ones. "Do not, for a moment, think this is your fault, Jez. It is not. This all comes back to greed, nothing short of. The greed of a mon who cannot leave it be."

'My grandfather?" It's weird saying this.

My grandfather. I have a grandfather.

I have a father.

"We believe so," Max confirms.

"But what has all this got to do with what's happening, or supposedly going to happen?" Cricket chirps up.

Placing both hands on his head, Max surveys everyone in the room.

"This goes no further than this room until we weed out the traitors in our midst, you hear me? I don't even know if I can trust the people in this room except my daughter and my VP," he says seriously.

There are a few disgruntled grumbles from my people.

"Other than your VP," I make a point of singling him out, staring straight into those ice blue eyes of his, then breaking the stare only to glance at Max, "And no offence Max, you too, there is no one in this room I do *not* trust. With my life."

"Then that is good enough for me." He shrugs. "Anyways, we digress. Striker contacted me, eventually, letting me know that he had you, and you were safe, so I began the processes to get myself and my club here. Now we are here, and I find my daughter, but not my friend. I find it hard to believe his death was an accident, the same as I don't believe Mouse's death was an accident. There have been too many *accidents* to be coincidence. Including that of my granddaughter."

All eyes turn to me when they hear my quick intake of breath.

"He knows?" Harmony asks, her eyes wide. "You told him?"

"Yes, I did Harms; he knows the whole story," I say softly to her. She knows I haven't spoken of the accident since it happened. "He deserved to know he had a granddaughter."

"Are you okay?" she asks, worry furrowing her brows and puckering her beautiful face.

"Never gonna be okay, but I'm breathing," I answer her honestly.

My heart hurts at the mention of my baby girl, but Max has not yet finished.

"So. Some people are looking over the accident reports again using a fine-tooth comb. We'll know soon if there are any discrepancies. Meanwhile, we need to be watchful, and Jez is not to go anywhere unescorted. Is that understood?" Max looks at my club members, *my family* as he states this.

"Now hang on a goddamn minute." I stand so quickly my chair makes a screeching noise as the legs scrape across the floor. "I'm *not* going to have a bodyguard twenty-four seven. Everyone has better things to do than to guard me from an invisible enemy. We don't even know for sure this guy knows where I am, and even if he does, *what the hell* would he want from me? I have nothing to give him."

"You can give him standing. You can give him an in with the Sanchez familia. Your mother was promised to Amelio Sanchez, but she ran. Debts must be paid. Promises must be kept. One of Diego Hernandez bloodline *must* wed one of the Sanchez bloodline. And you're the last one left." Ghost chimes in quietly, leaning forward in his chair, placing his hands, finger tips together on the table in front of him. "If he knows where you are, and these *accidents* tell me he does or he's close, he won't stop until you're where he thinks you belong. At the feet of the Sanchez men." His voice has a resigned sound to it, as if he believes it's only a matter of time before they come for me.

I don't want to believe this, but my body gives an involuntary shudder at the thought.

21

PLANS ARE MADE FOR MY SAFETY, DESPITE MY objections, and eventually everyone leaves the meeting room to get on with their day.

Lordy, Luke and a few others in the Broken Halos MC have a job in Las Vegas to tend to, so Cricket and Harmony have to redo the guard roster.

Lordy refuses to go initially, but Luke and I convince him everything is taken care of, and I'll be on my utmost best behavior and allow myself to be told what to do.

It's a lie, but I know Lordy won't go if I don't promise. We have signed agreements, so he has no choice, and he knows we don't break contracts. That's why we have such a trusted business name.

I'm on my way to the kitchen to grab a sandwich, when Blondie sidles up to me, slinking along next to me, like we're friends.

"So, Ghost and I talked the other night, and I think

he's ready to ask me to be his old lady. I thought you'd take it better coming from me. I know you run this club, and you know he isn't going to bow down to any woman. You wouldn't have time for someone like him anyway, and he needs constant attention. That big cock of his can go *allll* night long if you know what I mean." Blondie drags out the word all and finishes running her mouth with a stupid giggle.

I want to slap that snide look off her face.

Instead I go with my poker face and I'm proud that my voice doesn't show my anger. "You're more than welcome to him. Just make sure he doesn't try to swap spit with me again. Oh yeah," I add, "tell him to stop jerking off in the shower while calling my name, too." With that piece of juicy information, I walk into the kitchen, around the counter and open the fridge door, leaving her standing with her mouth hanging open.

Strange, but I seem to have lost my appetite.

Slamming the refrigerator door, I turn to stomp off to my room when I hit a brick wall.

"Whoa, where are you off to in a hurry?" Of course, it *has* to be him.

"Anywhere you aren't." I toss attitude at him.

"What am I supposed to have done now?" Ghost grumbles, his lips turned down, his eyebrows drawn together, and his eyes narrowed.

"Your new old lady came to let me down gently with the news. Doesn't think I'd be enough woman for you. She says the fact that I'm the prez wouldn't sit well with you anyway, as you couldn't be around a female in charge. I told her I was *fine* with that." I snap the last bit out like the crunch of a peanut brittle bar.

"I keep telling you, I don't have an old lady," he

grates out through clenched teeth, his eyes fading to icy blue.

I can't help myself; I *have* to poke the beast.

"Well she sure *thinks* she's about to become your old lady. You might want to let her in on that little fact. Blondie would fit right into your life just fine though. You have a big cock, and she has a big mouth. Match made in heaven if you ask me," I reply, trying to appear aloof, while all the time I can feel my body, *damned traitor*, reacting to the closeness of him.

His fist slams down on the counter next to me making me jump. Then he turns and storms out of the kitchen and I swear I heard him mumble something about putting me across his knee and paddling my backside.

Let him try.

The next few days are quiet; well, *relatively* quiet.

The Broken Halos try to get on with their routines without letting the Satans Vultures get in their way.

Lordy and the others won't be back at the compound for a few days yet, and Tinker's skulking around, looking lonely, so I challenge him.

I need a good workout, and everyone knows not to pull any punches in the ring, whether it's man to man, woman to woman, or mixed fighting. We have a proper ring setup in one of the barns.

At first, Tinker rejects my offer, but I keep digging at him until he gets a little riled and relents. I know he doesn't like fighting women, but I need the release.

This being on guard all the time and having to reign in my freedom is pissing me off.

I run upstairs and quickly dress in a black tank, and sports bra, *I may not have big breasts, but they get sore with the exercise when they bobble up and down constantly*. Besides that, they can be grabbed and twisted if they're not strapped down. I also change into a pair of lycra short shorts, and a pair of flip flops, which I'll kick off when I reach the barn. I leave my feet bare when I'm in the ring.

When I arrive at the barn, Tinker, dressed in a wife beater and boxer shorts, is already warming up, so I start my stretches also.

Once we're both ready, we enter the ring.

Although he's a little shorter than me at five feet seven inches, he's heavily built, and solid muscle. Lordy told me once that Tinker loves to wear women's silk underwear; that he likes the feel of them on his balls.

Too much information, right?

"Okay, Tinker show me whotcha got," I singsong to him as I thumb my nose and dance around the ring acting the clown.

Tinker crouches into a fighting stance, and tentatively swings a punch, which I avoid without a problem, then I drop to the floor and sweep his legs out from under him, so that he falls to the floor on his back. Once he's down, I twist to the side and bring my right elbow down in his solar plexus, hard. He makes a whooshing sound as the breath is forced from his body.

"C'mon man, you know better than that. Get your pussy ass up and let's do this for real. Otherwise you're gonna get an ass whuppin'." I try to imitate his Texan drawl, albeit badly.

As he gets to his feet, I signal with both my hands for

him to bring it, and as soon as he regains his breath, he does.

He feigns a roundhouse punch and as I duck he returns the favor, sweeping my legs out from under me, twisting my body as I fall so that my stomach hits the floor instead of my back. He now has his left arm around my neck and my right arm twisted up my back.

Fucker.

"Is this better, Jez?" he smugly whispers in my ear.

He thinks he has me.

Without warning, I throw my head back with as much force as I can, hitting him in the face. As Tinker weakens his grip I twist out from under him, rolling back and swinging my legs around his torso. I then use my body weight to roll the both of us so that I am under him, but he can't move as my legs are under his arms and he can't get a grip on me.

"Fuck!" he growls in frustration.

I am not essentially hurting him. He just can't move.

Releasing him from the hold, we both roll to our feet, but Tinker surprises me with a stomach punch which knocks the wind out of me. I go down like a sack of potatoes.

"Shit Jez," he thinks he genuinely hurt me and moves closer. "Are you okay? You said don't hold back." The look of concern on his face is endearing.

Sucker.

The moment he's close enough I punch him straight in the balls, and as he doubles over, I crack him in the jaw. Almost in slow motion, his body crumples to the floor.

Lights out.

Seizing a couple of towels and the bucket of water

next to them, I douse Tinker. He stirs straight away, and after shaking the water off and the fog of unconsciousness, he runs his hand over his face and looks at me.

"Why the fuck do you women always go for the balls? Every fucking time. Lucky Lordy's away or we'd both be in the doghouse." He gives them a good rub for effect.

"And yet you still leave them wide open for it." I grin, stretching out my hand to help him off the floor.

Tinker takes my offer of a hand up, but when I least expect it, he sweeps my feet out from under me, and pulls me into a sleeper hold.

"Can't trust anybody these days, Jez," he laughs as he tightens his grip and I begin to feel light headed.

Just as the world fades out I think I hear a familiar growl, "What the fuck?" and the floor to the ring vibrates as if something heavy landed on it.

Imagine my surprise when I open my eyes to find I'm lying on my bed with a damp cloth on my forehead.

Removing the cloth, I try to roll to the side of the bed to go pee, when I realize I have two long legs either side of me, two huge, muscled arms holding me in place, and when I tip my head back I discover my pillow is Ghost's chest.

"How you feelin'?" he murmurs.

I try to sit up, but his grip on me tightens.

"I'm fine. You can let me up now." I sound a little snippy, but that's me.

"You allowed one of your own people to knock you out with a sleeper hold. What the *fuck* were you thinking?" Ghost growls, his eyes narrowing, but he releases his hold on me.

"Lucky shot is all. I knocked his ass out before he got me back for it. I should've been prepared for it, so it's my bad." Now that I'm free of his hold I find I like the position I'm in, so I stay where I am. "What are you doing in my room, on my bed, and how did I end up in here?" I enquire.

"I carried you in here unconscious. You scared the motherfucking life outta me," he grunts, and as I look back up at him, his eyes begin to change to icy blue. "That motherfucker could've done some real damage. Do you or he realize that? Motherfucker's lucky I left him alive."

With that comment I shoot to a sitting position, twisting to face him, the cloth falling from my forehead.

"What motherfucker ... you mean Tinker?" Realization is slowly dawning on me. "What did you do to him? You better not have hurt him. I'll kick your ass if you did. *Fuck*!" I truly am worried with the thought that just ran through my head. "Lordy will *kill* you if you touched Tinker."

"He's fucking lucky Cricket came into the barn when she did, otherwise he'd be a dead man. She explained to me this is how you all get your kicks, stay fit and ready for action, and relieve tension. He's on my shit list though, and he knows he better not be getting' in that ring with you again." Ghost reaches for me, and in the beginning, I tense, but then I allow my body to relax, as he gently pulls me toward him, until we are chest to chest. He slides down my headboard at the same time as he pulls me onto him.

"W-What are you doing?" I question, gazing hypnotically into his blue eyes, that have now deepened to an ocean color, as my legs slide in between his.

Without answering, he continues to hold my gaze as he runs his thumb across my lower lip, then sliding his hand behind my head, pulls my lips to his gently. My eyes close, and I respond at the beginning without thinking. My brain kicks into gear and I pull back, but as I open my mouth to repeat the question, he pulls my lips to his again and his tongue enters my mouth, roughly tangling with mine.

He tastes of mint, and he smells like spice and leather.

Man, he can kiss.

Not that I'm exactly an expert; being up close and personal is not within my comfort zone, especially since my first, *my only*, real experience is one which caused me so much pain.

I won't be telling him that I have essentially no knowledge about dealing with men and sex.

It's none of his business anyway.

But kissing I can do. Kissing I enjoy.

With one hand on the back of my head, his other brushes down my body, up under my tank top and on to my back. His thumb brushes back and forth, moving lightly over my scars. I wait for him to say something about them, but he doesn't. My breasts become heavy and achy, and between my legs grows wet and warm.

These are strange sensations for me, unfamiliar, and I'm not sure what I want to do about it.

Breaking the kiss again, he gazes into my eyes, his irises darker than I've ever seen them.

"Sweet Jesus." His face has a confused expression,

and he cocks his head to one side as he continues to lock eyes with me. "What are you doing to me?" He whispers.

"What are you doing to *me*?" I repeat his words.

Suddenly Ghost's body tenses, and he rolls me off him, then immediately moves to the edge of the bed and gains his feet. His hands run through his hair, and he glances down quickly at me stating, "I'm sorry, I shouldn't have done that." Striding to the door, he opens it and leaves my room, closing the door behind him without another word.

The door shuts before my head clears itself of its fugue.

What the hell just happened?

What did I do wrong?

He touched my scars.

They're a part of me, and I have had to accept that.

The sick bastard who drugged and raped me, did a little knife work as well.

Plastic surgery could probably rid me of some of them, but they're part of who I am now, even though I don't flaunt them. They aren't something I'm proud to show off, if anything, it's the opposite, and now I know why. If I were naked, all anyone would see are tattoos, but if they were to run their hands over the designs, the scars would make themselves known.

Everyone's reaction is different, but Ghost's hurts like a bitch.

My eyes blur just for a moment before I allow the anger to settle within me again.

Fuck him!

22

Ghost makes a point of avoiding me.

Max makes a point of avoiding all conversation involving Ghost but ensures he and I have ample opportunity to get to know one another.

Cricket received a call to go into Las Vegas and help out Lordy, Luke and the others. *They needed a female point of view*, and since I was not able to go, she went.

Not wanting her to travel alone, I'm surprised when Hope volunteers to go with her. I'd rather it to be one of the guys, but I'd never admit that aloud, so Hope it is. To be on the safe side I ask Shadow to go as well. She'll be good backup if they need it.

I'm trying to catch up on some sleep when there's loud knocking on my door.

Checking my phone which sits on the dresser next to the bed, I see it's three a.m. in the morning.

There must be something wrong, I think as sleep recedes and panic sets in.

Crawling out from under the covers, for once still dressed in a tank top and panties, I step quickly to the door, unlock it, and pull it open.

Standing in my doorway, with tears running down her overly made-up face, her fake blonde hair mussed up, is none other than Blondie.

"What the fuck do you want?" I snarl at her. "Do you know what time it is?"

Fuck, I may not sleep much, but I was just about there.

"It's all your fault, you fucking slut," Blondie sobs. She genuinely seems distraught. "You couldn't fucking leave him alone, could you? You have your own fucking club, with your own men, but you had to take mine, didn't you. Harlot!" she yells. I see the slap coming and grasp her wrist before it connects with my face. Twisting her arm so it's up behind her back and holding it there with one hand, I use the other to push her face into the wall of the hall opposite my doorway. Blondie hits it so hard she puts a dent in the plaster with her face.

I have no idea why this is happening right now, but she just stepped over the line, so my care factor is currently zero.

I don't yell at her. I don't need to.

My voice is as cold as ice as I let her have it.

"Listen, you fucking nut case. I do not know, nor do I care what you're screeching about. But you just got your fucking ass kicked out of my compound. Do you understand me? I let you in as a courtesy to Lucifer, but you've now outstayed your welcome. You'll pack your bags and be the fuck off this compound before I get down to breakfast. Do you understand?"

Blondie appears visibly shaken by my cruel decision.

"You wouldn't." Her head twists to the side, eyes wide in disbelief, her voice now low, shaky, "My club members are here. I have no way of getting back to California without them. Ghost won't let you do this. Lucifer won't . . ."

I cut her off, "You don't get it do you? This is not *their* decision. Your ass is gone, and if they're not happy about it, they can go with you. I don't *give* a fuck. Now go pack your bags and Get. The. Fuck. Out." I emphasize my last words, so she knows I'm not fucking with her.

With that enlightenment, I let her go, stroll back into my room, and slam the door in her dazed face.

A few minutes go by when there's another knock on my door.

Jesus H, what part of that conversation did she not understand?

Do I need to beat it into her? Hmm, that might help me but not her.

I snatch the door open again, ready to let loose with another tirade, when I come to an abrupt halt.

Tinker is standing in my doorway, dressed simply in jeans, the rest of his body naked, including his feet, and no Stetson on his head. *And he has a black eye?* I know I split his lip, but I don't remember punching him in the eye.

Blondie is nowhere in sight.

He looks me over, "You okay? I heard the bitch yellin' ..." he drawls.

"I'm fine; she's been dealt with. How did you get a black eye? "I cut him off.

Blondie's predicament is the last thing on my mind now, as I go over our tussle blow by blow in my head.

Looking down at his feet, Tinker appears hesitant.

"Did I go crazy on you? If I did, I'm sorry Tinker, but I don't remember. That hasn't happened in quite a while …"

"No … No, it wasn't you, it was …" he breaks into my thoughts, then trails off before finishing the sentence, as if he doesn't want to tell me.

I watch him chew the inside wall of his mouth nervously, his eyes avoiding mine.

Now I'm truly getting pissed. Someone else touched one of my people?

"Who was it Tinker? Tell me right now. No bullshit!" I snap.

He knows I won't be pussy-footed around with now.

"Your boyfriend did it. Ghost. But you can't blame him, he thought we were fighting for real, and when he saw you in my sleeper hold, and you were passed out, he hauled off and punched me. Then he picked you up and carried you up here. He musta thought he was protectin' you from me." His verbal diarrhea ends, with him looking sheepish, a wry grin on his face. "I was out fuckin' cold before I hit the mat, Cricket reckons."

"Ghost is *not* my *boyfriend* or any other kind of friend." My lip curls up into a sneer. "He is the Satans Vultures VP, nothing else, and he does *not* have the right to hit *anyone* in my club."

Who does the asshole think he is?

I don't need protection from my own people, especially *his*.

"Go back to bed, Tinker, see you in the morning. Make sure Blondie is escorted off this compound. I want her gone. Understood?"

My word is law, even if this is a democratic club.

All I get in acknowledgement is a nod of Tinker's head, as he turns and pads barefoot back up the hallway to his room.

I close the door and hesitate a few moments behind it in case someone else wants to know what the fuss is all about, but there are no more knocks.

Padding barefoot to my bed, I huff as I plop my body back down on it, my brain going over the last half hour.

Blondie deserved what she got tonight. She's lucky it's so early in the morning, or she would have got an ass kicking to go with being tossed out of the compound.

Tinker, however, *that* is another matter, and as I mull over the conversation with him, I can feel my anger building.

How *dare* Ghost take it upon himself to hit one of my people. Who the fuck gave him permission?

What did he think was going to happen when he started kissing and touching me, and why did I respond like I did? Why did he stop?

Why am I thinking about that now?

His hot and cold temperament is confusing, and it pisses me off even more because it *does* bother me.

I tell myself I'm angry about Ghost hitting one of my people, but I know it also has to do with what happened in my room earlier. The longer I stare at the door to the bathroom, which I know has another exit that leads to Ghost's room, the more my temper flares.

Not even thinking about the fact that it's now three-thirty a.m. in the morning, and he'll be asleep, *if he isn't fucking one of his club whores*, I slide off the bed, and storm to the bathroom door. I kept my side locked after the kissing incident, so I unlock it, open the door, and enter the bathroom.

The thought hasn't even crossed my mind that his door may be locked from his side.

It isn't.

Was he hoping his kisses would make me so needy that I wouldn't be able to resist him, so he left the door open for when I ran to him and begged him for more?

Huh? Where the fuck are these thoughts coming from?

Tinker. Black eye. Asshole.

Stay on track, Jez.

Entering the room, I flick the light switch on, not feeling sorry for the man at all, expecting Ghost to bolt upright in bed, confused and momentarily blinded by the sudden brightness.

Imagine my surprise when he lays his arm across his eyes and growls, "I don't know how no one has been able to find you all this time, Jez. You make enough noise to wake the fucking dead."

"Well, ha fucking ha," I give him sarcasm. "You're a funny man, aren't you." It isn't a question. Glaring at him with my *if looks could kill face*, I point my finger at him, noticing my hand's shaking with ... anger? "Who gave you the right to come into my compound and hit my people?"

Ghost reaches under the sheet he has covering his lower torso, pulling a Beretta 92FS 9mm semi auto pistol, ten shot, out from under it, and casually places it on the nightstand next to the bed

He sleeps with a gun?

Meh. I sleep with a razor under my pillow.

Whatever floats his boat.

Glancing in the direction my gaze was currently directed at, he replies, "You never know when you might need it in a hurry." As if bored, he sighs, reaches up behind his head and holding onto the headboard of the bed with both hands, pulls his giant body up into a sitting position, similar to the one he sat in on my bed, when he held me close between his legs.

My eyes widen, and my throat goes dry as I watch his muscles in his arm and chest tense and flex with the movement.

His chest is bare of tattoos. The position he's in shows off his enormously wide shoulders and his pecs. His six pack is bunched just right and blondish hair trails from his belly button down under the sheet. Judging by the sheet covering his remaining parts, the rest of him is in the buff also. I try not to linger too long on the bulge at his crotch, forcing my eyes upward.

What was I here for again?

The muscles in his arms swell as he remains holding onto the bedhead, and as my gaze settles on his face, his lips twitch with a smirk.

"See something you like?" the cocky prick asks softly.

Wait.

What?

No. I was angry.

I *am* angry

Spitting mad even.

"You punched one of my people," I spit out.

Ghost heaves a sigh.

"I punched your man because he had you in a sleeper hold, and you were out cold. How was I to know you spar like that, with no holds barred? Against men. Do you realize how much damage can be inflicted like that? I thought he had genuinely hurt you. If it hadn't been for Cricket, I probably would have taken him out."

He would have killed Tinker?

"Why would you *do* that?" I snark, confused. "You'd be sentencing yourself to death. Lordy would not rest until you *were*, and besides, Tinker wouldn't exactly have laid down for you."

"I did it because I thought Tinker hurt you. I apologized to him when he came to, but I also told him I'd do it again if I found the fucker in the same position as I did."

Now *he* sounds angry.

I lock onto those ice blue eyes, taking in his too handsome face, noting the tick in his jaw.

"What the fuck are *you* angry about?" I snap. "*I'm* the one who should be angry. When you're in my compound you'll follow the rules like everyone else around here. Do you hear me?" As I stomp my foot hard on the floor, I realize how childish it seems.

"I'm pissed because it's now four in the morning, and I was sleeping, until a certain tall, sexy woman stormed into my damned room wearing nothing but a tank top and satin panties, angry because I was trying to protect her. I'm angry because said sexy tall woman now has my cock hard as a rock," he grinds out as he adjusts himself with his left hand.

My gaze falls unwillingly to the sheet. Yep, it is. It is *definitely* hard.

Ghost continues, "But I know the last thing on your mind is letting me fuck you, so if you aren't gonna help me out here, at least get out so I can get a handle on it." He reaches under the sheets for his cock, and he wraps his large hand around it, giving it a pump, as if that might relieve the problem.

My lips forms an O.

I look down at myself quickly. In my haste to berate him I forgot what I was wearing, I was so angry at him.

"So? You going to come on over here and help me out, Jez?" Ghosts voice sounds huskier than usual, and my eyes watch as he pumps his cock again.

My mouth is dry, but between my legs is wet. I can feel it.

My heart's thumping so hard, it feels like it wants to jump out of my chest.

"I can smell you from here, Jez. I know how turned on you are. Either you get your ass over here and in this bed or get the fuck out and let me take care of this myself. What's it gonna be?" he asks again in that same voice.

My body wants to go and get in the bed with him, but my brain is screaming *sex is pain*.

I may not remember much about my rape, but I do remember how much pain my body was in afterwards.

Licking my dry lips, I stare into his now ocean blue ones.

"I … can't. I can't," I repeat, my eyes becoming glassy with tears. My voice is barely a whisper as I turn and flee back to my room. Ensuring the door is safely bolted from my side, I jump into my bed and let the tears that I've been holding in flow, only to be let out in private.

Ghost doesn't want a freak like me. He just needed a release.

Bob doesn't care that I'm a freak, so when I've finished with the tears I reach into my dresser drawer and take him out. Imagining Ghost with his hand pumping his big cock helps me orgasm almost instantly. Feeling exhausted, I allow myself to drift off to sleep for an hour before I have to get up again and start my day.

23

"JEZ, WHAT THE HELL HAPPENED LAST NIGHT?" MAX asks as I enter the kitchen around six a.m.

He is seated at the kitchen table, with the chair turned backward.

"Good morning to you too, *Dad*." It's unfamiliar on my tongue. "Don't you know how to sit on a chair properly? What do you mean what happened last night?" My face burns as I think about being in Ghost's room and his blatant offer of sex.

How did Max find out?

Did Ghost tell him?

"I heard you told Sugar to pack her shit and piss off back to California. What did she do now?" Max growls.

Relief swamps me as what he's talking about sinks in

.

"Yep." I pop the P. "That bitch was warned not to start shit in my house, and she went and did it anyway. Banging on my door at three in the fucking morning screeching about me taking her man. She can get gone, and if any of you don't like it, *Dad*," I hiss, "you all can go *with* her."

I calmly walk over to the table carrying my coffee cup, with the *Team Grizz* logo, and seat myself opposite him.

My face is blank, but my heart picks up a little. My brain wants his approval for some reason. I need to know I've done the right thing sending her away.

Max's face turns into a grimace as he throws back the last dregs of his coffee. He begins to stand, then seats himself again and reaches across the table grasping my hand that is not holding my cup. I allow him this. He *is* trying. I can see that.

"Jez, this is your territory, your club, and your compound. I would never ask you to change a decision that's in yours and your people's best interest. Ghost's gonna run her into Las Vegas and put her on a bus for California, or wherever the fuck she wants to go. She's a sweet butt, nothing more, nothing less. Sugar knows this, and if any of her buddies chime in, they can go with her. We are here for *you*, not them."

With that statement he lets go of my hand, stands, turns the chair around to its correct position, pushes it under the table, and leaves me sitting alone with my coffee.

I don't really understand why, but I'm pleased he abides by my decision.

I don't know why it has to be Ghost, who takes Blondie aka Sugar into Las Vegas, and I sulkily watch from the clubroom doorway as she tearfully says her goodbyes to her friends. Rosie is crying. She must love that bitch, though I have no idea why. I think Blondie tries to get Max to override my decision, as she clings to him, and gives him a pleading expression. Max shakes his head, and although I'm not close enough to hear what's said, I hear her sob as he shakes his head again and leads her to where Ghost sits on his bike, waiting.

For a moment I feel a little guilt, but that disappears when Blondie unexpectedly looks over to where I'm standing and screams at the top of her lungs, "You'll get yours, *slut*. You think that getting me outta the way will get you to being Ghost's old lady? It won't. I hope you die, you whore. I *hate* you."

What is she, twelve?

While she's screaming abuse at me, Max picks her up bodily and practically throws her on the seat behind Ghost, meanwhile Ghost is revving his engine trying to drown her out. When that doesn't work, he spins around, grabs her by her hair and says something in her ear. I can't see his face, but I can see hers. It goes pale, she stops screeching, and begins sobbing. Blondie then places her hands around Ghost's waist and buries her face in the back of his cut.

I wish it were me on the back of his bike.

What is *up* with that?

The bike is moving now, and the gate to the compound rolls open to allow it through.

As it picks up speed, the bike motor gives out a low rumble that I love to hear, then it fades away as the pair roll on down the road.

I know Las Vegas is not far from the compound, but it seems like days before Ghost arrives back without his passenger, although it's no more than a couple of hours. He must have waited with her for the bus. I asked Max why they didn't put her on a plane to send her back, and he told me Blondie has a morbid fear of flying. Maybe that's what Ghost threatened her with when she was tossing her threats at me earlier.

Ghost hasn't spoken a word to me, and I wonder fleetingly if he got Blondie in to help him with his hard on last night as a kind of goodbye.

***

I've not been able to bring myself to try sex since I was raped, though I have watched a lot of porn.

I have given head, well sort of, just to one man, and I have been on the receiving end of being eaten out, but it was in the dark, and I was so tense the whole time I don't know whether I enjoyed it or not.

Striker tried to get me back in the game, as he called it, but I couldn't deal with it, so he left me alone after that.

He was a lot older than me, probably close to Max's age and I felt nothing for him but gratitude for taking me with him when my grams was killed in the fire, but I felt safe enough with him to try to let him show me that sex shouldn't be scary or painful.

It didn't work.

Everyone assures me that it's not meant to be painful, and if it is, then the person you are having it with definitely doesn't know what they are doing, but I can't get past the fear.

Cricket and Striker tried futilely to get me to go to a therapist for help, but I stubbornly refused.

Harmony tells me an orgasm is as good as eating chocolate, but Bob has given me plenty of orgasms, plus I've eaten plenty of chocolate, and I don't see the similarity.

Why am I even thinking about sex, I groan inwardly? Am I that frustrated that I'm truly considering it?

———

It has been a few days since the Blondie incident, and I'm sitting alone in my office downstairs when I google the word sex.

Clicking on images, I study some of them. In each image they twosome, sometimes threesome, and oh my gawd, a *foursome?*... It's something to behold.

Clicking on a link that takes me to a porn site, I click on a video and watch for a while. Both the male and female are ham actors, but they look like they truly enjoy what they are doing.

Maybe it's time for me to try again.

I don't know.

The thought thrills me and scares the shit out of me all at once.

Buzzing brings me out of my head.

I hit the intercom button.

"Yeah?"

Tinker's voice comes through the system, "Jez, you need to get up here, stat. We got a sit-rep."

When Tinker starts using military jargon I know we

have trouble, so I immediately get to my feet and head upstairs, without even closing off the laptop.

No code is needed from the inside, so I quickly open the door and enter the hall. Arriving in the clubhouse common room, I see people crowded around something on the floor.

Parting the sea of bodies, I openly gasp at the sight before me.

Lying on a blanket on the floor of my clubhouse is a body, or parts of a body. The hands and feet are missing. There's so much blood that it's hard to distinguish whether it's male or female despite the fact that it's naked. The facial features have been beaten to a pulp.

Then I see it through the dirt and dry caked blood. The tattoo.

"It's Sugar," I state matter-of-factly, shocked that this bloodied bruised thing was a human being a few days ago.

There are gasps as the others who knew her learn of her identity.

Rosie collapses to the ground beside her friend and sobs, moaning, "No ... No."

Sugar has been tortured, you can see why she is so hard to recognize. More than likely the sick fuck or fuckers who did this probably raped her too. I hated the bitch, but I feel a wave of guilt at having made her leave the compound merely to be viciously murdered by what must be animals, for surely no human could do that to a defenceless woman.

My stomach does a somersault as I realize I played a part in her death.

Two large hands grasp my shoulders.

"Don't you dare." I hadn't realized Ghost was behind me until he spoke softly in my ear. "Don't you even think for a second that this is on you. You did not do this. These evil pricks must be watching every move we make to know how to get one of us alone. I swear she got on that bus. They must have been waiting at one of the stops for her to go to the bathroom or something. But you do not blame yourself, you hear?"

I nod absently, but I know in my heart this is all my fault. If I hadn't been jealous over her wanting to be with Ghost, I probably wouldn't have tossed her out to the wolves.

"She was never with me and was never going to be, Jez. Don't torture yourself." Again, he's inside my head, reading my thoughts.

At the same time, Rosie looks up at me, tears streaming down her face, and points her finger at me wailing, "This is on *you*. You were jealous of her. You couldn't stand the fact that she was going to be Ghost's old lady, so you threw her out on her own to get rid of her."

I can't be angry at the inconsolable young woman, sitting beside the dismembered body of her friend.

Besides, she is right in one way.

"I'm sorry," is all I can give her right now.

I turn and walk away, tears pushing their way into my eyes, blurring my escape to a place where no one can see me cry.

I'm in a daze as I scan my keycard, punching in the code for the basement. It's not until I find myself standing in the middle of my office, I realize Ghost is still with me.

"You shouldn't be here," I hear myself say, my voice seeming to come from a distance.

"You shouldn't be alone right now," he growls back as he steps up behind me and pulls my back to his chest then wraps his arms around me. "Let it out Jez. I got you girl."

At those words I let the tears flow. I don't know why, but I don't care right now if he sees me break. My body trembles and my legs weaken.

"I got you," Ghost whispers softly as he gathers me into his arms like I weigh nothing and walks us over to my big black leather office chair. He sits down and pulls me close to his chest. One arm holds me in place, the other rubs my back soothingly, drawing imaginary circles on the base of my spine.

Meanwhile I'm seated on his lap, gripping his cut with both hands, the side of my face glued to his pecs, my knees pulled up to my chest, as I let myself cry. I don't care right now that there are tears running down his chest and I don't think he does either. Sometime during my snot fest, I must have fallen asleep, and I waken to the realization that I'm now in my own bed. My eyes, which are swollen from crying, try to open, and I let out a groan as my head thumps with a tension headache.

Needing to pee, I try to roll off the bed, but a large hand reaches around my body and pulls me backward.

Ghost is in the bed with me.

Again.

I let him pull me close, and snuggle my back into his chest, feeling the heat of his body permeate mine. That niggling familiarity of his scent permeates my nose again, but I can't put my finger on the memory.

I also feel the raging hard-on he has crushed up against my backside, and I purposely wriggle my ass.

"Don't do that, Jez, if you don't mean it." Sleepy, Ghost grumbles. "I'm hanging on by a thread here, so if you don't want me to fuck you, then be good and lay still. It'll go away. I hope," he adds.

24

My body tenses involuntarily, and I hate it for doing that.

I need to forget.

The tension has been caused by my situation, the pain of losing my little girl, the fear I have inside me, and my guilt for the death of Sugar.

Why is it I can only call her by her club name after she's dead?

I need to forget that too.

"You're in your head again, Jez. Stop it and talk to me," Ghost grumbles, tightening his grip around my waist.

How is he reading my thoughts?

"I need to go to the bathroom," I say in response.

My body is reacting to the closeness, and I need to put some space between us.

"Nope, Jez, you're not leaving this bed, okay? If I let you go now, you'll simply run." He grunts in my ear.

The fucker's fully awake now and pissing me off,

because he's got that voodoo, mind reading shit happening.

"Stop it," I snap.

"Stop what?" Ghost askes innocently.

"Stop reading my bloody mind," I snarl.

"Jez, relax. We won't do anything that makes you uncomfortable. Except talk. Now I *know* that makes you uneasy. Hell, it makes *me* uneasy too, but it needs to be done." Ghost is speaking quietly, soothingly, almost like he's trying to calm a skittish cat, and I force my body to relax, by taking a deep breath, in through my nose and out through my mouth.

"I know this is your MC, your compound, but hear me out before you make any further decisions, please. We need to step up security, and we need to bring your people home where we can protect each other from these animals. Where are they anyway?" Ghost rolls my body toward him, so we are face to face, but doesn't let go of me.

"They're working. We have businesses to run, contracts to fill, and they can't just walk away from them. We have a name to uphold, and it's how we make our money. Once this contract is done in a few days, they will all come back together. Safety in numbers." I'm a little embarrassed to tell him we earn our money mostly legally, unlike a lot of clubs.

Unlike Striker, who dealt on both sides of the law, but mainly on the wrong side.

"What contracts? With whom? Don't you think your club is more important than contracts?" He isn't going to back off on this.

Taking a deep breath, then releasing it slowly, I tell him.

"We own several security companies, dealing with everything from private bodyguards to the rich and famous, to tracking bail skips. Mainly around the Las Vegas area, but extending into Phoenix and surrounding cities. Depending on the contract, it might be just a one-person job, or we may all be involved. Sometimes we can be gone for days, sometimes weeks. The contracts are exclusive and pay very well." I find myself blushing as I look into his eyes to gauge his reaction to my revelation.

I'm telling him a half-truth. He doesn't need to know that we also find people, mostly missing kids, and teens that sometimes only people without the invisible strings of red tape can find.

We may look like merely a bunch of bikers to the outside world, and other clubs, but we're extremely close-knit and have mostly honest ways of making our living.

Holding my gaze, Ghost moves so close to my face that his lips are almost brushing mine. His minty breath flows up my nasal passages as I inhale.

"So, you're not really a bunch of badasses after all?" He chuckles.

His comment pisses me off, and I try to roll away from him. "You can leave right *now*," I snarl.

Not badass? I'll show *him* badass!

"Oh no you don't, Jez. You're staying right here." Ghost tries to tighten his grip on me, and I bring my knee up to connect with his balls. Instead of connecting though, my leg is knocked sideways, and I'm suddenly tossed onto my back, my legs parted by one of his, as he slides right between them as if he belongs there.

My hands instinctively become claws and I try to rake his face with my nails, but he's too fast, locking both my wrists in one big hand, forcing them up above my head.

My chest's heaving, with anger and frustration at being bested by anyone, especially him.

"Get the fuck off me. *Now,*" I snarl at him.

"Nuh uh. Not gonna happen Jez. So take a chill pill and calm the fuck down. If I let you go, that razor in your boot is gonna be at my throat the second I relax, and I like being a live ghost, not a real one." He smirks at his own joke.

I glare at him. He is not in the least bit funny.

Ghost's expression turns from teasing to serious, "I'm sorry Jez, okay? I didn't mean to make light of your club. I admire the fact that you have businesses that are above-board and make you good money. Stop fighting me, please."

His eyes show he is telling the truth, so I force myself to calm down, letting my body relax.

As I do, I realize Ghost is hard. His cock I mean, but then his body is too. There doesn't appear to be an ounce of fat on his whole frame.

Except maybe his head.

I smile at my own joke.

"What are you smiling at?" he asks in that same husky voice I remember from his bedroom when I stormed in to rip him a new asshole for giving Tinker a black eye.

The night I sent Sugar packing.

Damn, I didn't want to go back there, and the guilt starts to filter in again.

"You, Jez, are a complicated woman. One second you fight me, then you're smiling, then you let yourself get in your head and we are back to square one. I only know one remedy for that." Ghost growls as he leans down and kisses me.

I refuse to enter into his game for a few seconds, until he runs his tongue along my bottom lip, and without my permission, my mouth opens and allows his tongue to enter it and tangle with mine.

Traitorous mouth.

My body begins to respond to his, and I feel the clenching of my lower parts and the electricity that seems to be running through me. My panties become wet as I allow myself to succumb to his nips at my lips and his caressing of my breasts with the tips of his fingers. An involuntary moan escapes in between his kisses, and it slowly registers this comes from me.

"Jez, I'm gonna let go of your hands now, okay?" Ghost's husky voice whispers in my ear, and I nod in acceptance. "If you tell me to stop, Jez, it's gonna kill me, but I will stop," he assures me in a soothing tone. "I want to take your top off. Is that okay?"

Our eyes meet as he looks to me for my permission, and I frown with indecision as I think of the scars that cover parts of my body. Will he notice in the dusky light?

"Jez, you need to use your words." He grasps my chin, bringing my face to his and kissing me gently on the tip of my nose.

"Yes, y-yes it's okay." It's shaky but positive.

My arms willingly stay above my head as Ghost rolls to the side for a moment while he pulls my tank top up and I roll with him to take it over my head. As soon as he has it off, he tosses it somewhere over his shoulder, and I think fleetingly of what Hope will say if she has to pick my clothes up off the floor. I forget about that as quickly as I think of it when Ghost lowers his head to my bra clad breasts. I am thankful that I have a preference for nice satin bras and panties to match.

Thanks Grams, I say silently in my head.

She used to say that in case I ever got hit by a bus, I should ensure my bra and panties matched. The satin part I decided on later.

His mouth closes over my nipple from the outside of my bra, and he bites down, not hard enough to hurt, but enough to send an electric current down between my legs.

If I thought I was wet before, I'm soaked now.

"Ghost?" I groan.

I get no answer.

"Ghost?" I try again

"Hmmm?" is my lone response as he bites down on my other nipple.

"I … I … oh sweet Jesus," I moan aloud, as he lowers my bra cup enough to squeeze my nipple with his fingers.

"What Jez? Tell me what you want? I need to hear you say it," he croons smoothly.

"I have to tell you some things before we … you know … do this." I'm finding it hard to concentrate on what I'm trying to say, but it's important.

"I haven't … well other than when I was … well, that's the one time I've had …" My body tenses up when I can't find the words I need to say. The words that might mean Ghost will stop creating the incredible sensations he's causing in my body right now. He probably won't want to touch me after this, but I need to get it out.

Ghost stops and raises his head, so we are eye to eye again.

His eyes are practically royal blue now.

"You can tell me, Jez, but it won't have any bearing on what's happening between us right now, unless you want me to stop. Do you want me to stop?"

I stare into his eyes. "No, maybe … I don't know. I don't want you to stop, but you might not want to continue once I tell you this." I can't keep his gaze any longer, and close my eyes, preparing to find myself alone once I've told him.

Ghost sighs as he once again rolls to the side, catches my chin in his hand, and turns me to face him. "Eyes on me, Jez. Talk to me. I'm here. I'm listening, and I'm not going anywhere unless you want me to." He leans forward, placing a soft kiss on my lips, then leans away, waiting for me to talk.

I'm trying hard not to get up and run, but that is what my mind wants me to do.

As if he senses it, Ghost rolls onto his back, pulling me into him, laying my head on his chest, and wrapping his arm around me.

His hand is drawing circles on my skin, and it somehow relaxes me.

Clearing my throat, I tell my story, or part thereof.

"I haven't been with anyone, ever, like this. Other than when I was … well, you know the story. Not before. Not since. I was a virgin when it all happened. The one good thing that came out of it was Marley. And now I don't even have her. Striker tried to help me, but I froze every time he touched me. Everyone tried to talk me into seeing a counselor, but I haven't been able to bring myself to talk about it. The only time I *have* talked about what happened to me to anyone, other than Nitro, Cricket and Harmony, was when I told Max." I don't add that if I'd realized Ghost was there, I would've clammed up. "It brought everything back, everything I have tried so hard to lock away. My club needs me to be strong, to be their leader. I cannot become the basket case I was. They don't need me falling apart again, and I refuse to do it. I live with the scars that animal gave me, on my body, but also in my head on a daily basis. It's okay if you can't deal with either of them. I understand if this is all you want from me. Believe me when I say, I want this too, with you, but know that I won't hold it against you if you can't deal with it." I hiccup a sob as I finish, as I'm expecting Ghost to roll off the bed and leave the room again. I close my eyes, so I don't have to watch him go.

Seconds stretch into minutes, and when there's no movement from Ghost, I open my eyes again, and look up at him.

He's still here holding me.

I try to sit up, but his arm is like a vice around my body, so I still my efforts.

"*Fuck. Fuck. Fuck.* If I could get near that *motherfucker*, I'd kill him with my bare hands. I can't believe there was no trace of his DNA in the network. I give you my word, Jez. I won't rest until that fucker is dead and rotting in hell; after he's felt some of his own pain." Ghost's eyes are glued to the ceiling. One hand is in his hair gripping it tight, and his jaw is ticking with his anger.

I believe he *would* kill my attacker if he could find him.

"There has never been any trace of him. Nitro even called in markers, but she got nothing, I whisper softly. "I understand if all this turns you off."

25

GHOSTS EYES RETURN TO MINE, AND HIS FACE softens.

"I'm sorry all this's happened to you Jez, and I know you aren't out of the woods yet. But don't you think for one minute that I don't want you. I tried to fight it, but I knew from the moment I laid eyes on you again, it was a losing battle."

With that comment, Ghost rolls me to my back once more, and moving with me, he slides his big frame between my legs again. Strangely, I feel comforted in the fact that we seem to fit together perfectly.

His face closes the distance between us, and he kisses me. Gently at first, but when he feels me respond, it deepens, becoming a crushing, bruising, passionate kiss that seems to pour his feelings out of his body and into mine.

I don't feel him undo my bra, and it isn't until he moves his head lower to grasp my nipple in his teeth I realize it has happened. After sliding the bra from my arms, then dropping it to the floor, his hands grasp mine, and with our fingers entwined, he moves them once more up above my head.

Leaving my swollen lips, his head lowers, and I feel his teeth graze first one nipple, hardening it to a virtually painful but electric state, then he moves to the other and continues the onslaught. He doesn't seem to hesitate as his hands run over the many small scars that litter my torso.

My body is catching fire, and I can't help but squirm beneath him as I feel the current running from my breasts to between my legs. I can vaguely hear moans, and it shocks me to realize they're mine. My legs try to clench together, but Ghost has his body between them, so I attempt to ease the tension in my pelvis by rubbing against his still clothed body like a wanton whore.

Repeating the words he'd said before our heart to heart, the husky voice of Ghost penetrates the haze he has me writhing in as he twists and plucks my nipples, squeezing and pinching, giving me pleasure with a little pain.

"Tell me what you want, Jez, use your words. I need to hear you say them."

"Please, Ghost." I have no idea what I'm pleading for, simply that I need something. Relief of some kind.

Ghosts face appears through my haze, his deep blue eyes feel like they are gazing down into my soul.

"Please what, Jez? What do you want?" he prompts me again.

"Please, I want you … I need you … oh don't stop. Please." Knowing I'm begging for him to do something, anything to ease this pressure that's building in me is in my *I don't care* file right now. I need … *more*.

Letting go of my hands Ghost sits back on his haunches for a moment, and I panic, thinking he's leaving me again. Raising my head, I watch as he grasps both sides of my beautiful satin and lace panties and tears them from my body. Scowling at him, I huff "You are so replacing those. They were my favorites."

Meanwhile my heart is thudding so hard I can hear it, and a sheen of sweat coats my body.

"If I have my way you won't be wearing any under-wear ever again," he replies with a mischievous grin and a wink.

I know in my heart he is placating the freak, while he gets what he wants. He will tire of my idiosyncrasies soon enough and move on.

Ghost stands beside the bed and slowly removes his cut, folds it, and lays it on the dresser, while I relish in the vision of his bare torso. Gasping a little at the sight, I note that both his nipples are pierced. Both have a silver bar with small balls either end sitting horizontally. I want to touch them but don't. His belt is undone now, and he's commando beneath his black skinny leg jeans, as he lets them fall around his feet, then steps out of them. Socks and boots had already been removed before we started this … whatever it is.

Watching in awe, I can't believe the size of his cock as it springs free of his jeans, *and* he has a piercing.

Oh. My. God in sweet heaven.

That thing is going to hurt.

Ghost curses when he sees my rounded eyes and my teeth chewing my lower lip, as he realizes I'm scared.

Terrified more like it.

He pulls me to the edge of the bed into a sitting position, with my feet hanging over the edge. Leaning over me his hand cups my chin as he raises my face toward his.

"Hey, hey, Jez, look at me. We can stop any time. You don't have to do this if you aren't ready. I know you're expecting pain, and I won't tamp it down for you. There may be some, but I'll try not to cause you any more than you can handle. Because you haven't had a man touch you without pain, you'll tense up. But I need you to try not to. I'm going to show you how good it can feel, okay? Jez?" His voice is soothing, but my brain is still on his huge cock and piercing.

"Jez? Do you want to stop this? Just say the word." Ghost sounds worried that I'm not answering him.

I tried to give Striker head once, but I wasn't very good, and kept my eyes closed the whole time, so I had never had a good look at a cock up close. Though I watch porn, it's not quite the same in reality.

Raising my eyes to his I ask such a virgin question, blushing as I do.

"Can I touch it?" I whisper so quietly I'm not sure he hears me.

Instead of laughing at me, Ghost reaches for my hand and guides it to his solid cock, clasping my hand firmly on it. He hisses and rolls his head back on his shoulders.

I look up into his face. He looks so beautiful. His head now dips toward me and I can see his eyes are hooded, and his mouth is slightly parted. His tongue sweeps his lower lip causing it to glisten.

Ghost still has my hand under his and gives his huge cock a hard pump, causing him to shudder.

Returning my eyes to what's in front of me I notice

his cock makes my hand look small and I can't get my fingers all the way around it. There are purplish veins running in uneven lines up and down his shaft, and they're pulsating, I can feel them on my palm. Under the head, at the top, is his piercing. A ring with several small silver balls on it enter the stem of his cock and exit out the head, or maybe it's the other way around.

I have to ask.

"Did that hurt?" I look up to see him watching me.

Ghost shrugs. "The Prince Albert? Like a bitch."

"So why do it?"

Another dumb question.

"Because I was young and dumb at the time, but I kept it when I found out how good it makes women feel when I fuck them," he answers without missing a beat.

I bet Sugar enjoyed it, I think to myself.

His cock jumps in my hand as if to bring me back to earth, and I continue my study of it. The head itself is purplish and angry looking, as if it wants to explode, and on top of that, above the exit, *or entrance*, of the Prince Albert his slit has pre-cum seeping out. For some reason I want to taste it, so I lean forward and touch it with my tongue. It tastes a little salty but good.

Ghost lets out a groan and I jump back afraid I've hurt him.

'I'm sorry, I didn't mean to hurt you," I apologize quickly.

"Jez, you have nothing to apologize for. You didn't hurt me. I loved that you wanted to taste me. It felt good." His voice is deep and husky now, and his words spur me on.

I lick his cock again, feeling the heat of it on my

tongue. He hisses, and reaches down with one hand, enclosing it over mine again.

"Grip it like this," he squeezes my hand a little to increase my pressure on the base of his cock, slides my hand up and down his shaft a few more times, and I hear his breathing hitch.

"Do you want me to fuck that sweet mouth of yours, Jez? Open up and I'll guide you through it." Ghost growls, and automatically I open my mouth, although my mind is screaming *it ain't gonna fit girl*, at me.

"We'll do this together Jez, slow and steady. If you can't do it, it's okay. Relax your throat, that'll help with the gag reflex." He's trying to keep me in the moment.

Acting on reflex, I reach out with my tongue, swirling it around the purplish head, ending with his slit which has more precum on it. I force my mouth to relax and slide my lips around the head and down the stem of his engorged cock, trying to relax my throat like he said.

"Jez? Jesus, Jez?" I look up at him as he growls my name. "It feels so good, but can you back off with your teeth a bit baby, they're damned sharp." Ghost winces, although he also has a sort of smile on his face at the same time.

Shit, I didn't realize.

I pop his cock out of my mouth to apologize.

"I'm sorry. I told you I sort of haven't done this before. Maybe we should stop ..." I'm looking down at the floor, biting both my lips, and blushing like a schoolgirl.

"Hey now. Jez? Hey, look at me, woman." He reaches down and lifts my chin with one hand, and I slowly raise my eyes to his. "I didn't expect it is all, Jez. You didn't hurt me, not really, just grazed me. Cocks are a little more sensitive than other parts of the body, the same as between your legs is. You want to try again?" He sounds like he is placating a child.

Ghost must really want to fuck the freak, maybe so he can feel good about himself, or maybe because he knows he won't have Sugar any more.

I'm feeling disconnected. The moment is over. The feelings I was having before are subsiding, and I'm beginning to wallow in self-pity and guilt again.

"I think we should forget it. I'm a freak. You need someone who knows what they're doing. Not some twenty-six-year-old woman who doesn't know what to do with a man," I mumble, as I stand, intending to get dressed.

"Whoa, what the fuck, Jez?" Ghost grasps me by the shoulders as I try to walk past him to find my clothes. Forcing my chin up with one hand, he demands, "Jez, look at me."

I don't want to. There'll just be disappointment in his eyes, like Striker's when *he* tried to *help* me.

"You need to go." My voice is flat, and I refuse his demand, my gaze still to the floor. Right now, I feel like shit. Once again, I'm the freaky woman who can't have real sex with a real person. Bob will have to do it for me for the rest of his battery-operated life. At least Bob can't tell me how disappointing I am.

"It's okay, Ghost. Freaks like me can't be fixed with a fuck. I know this. I need you to leave." I sigh. My voice becomes stronger with my conviction. "*Now.*"

I pull out of his grip, walk to the door, open it, and hold onto it. He doesn't need to know how much my legs are shaking, or how much I hate myself for the way I am.

Ghost's face is expressionless as he pulls his jeans on

without zipping or buttoning them. Bending over he grabs his boots. He looks inside them, then around the room, homing in on his socks. He dresses in his cut, looks around the room again as if he's missing something, shrugs, then leaves.

As I'm about to close the door, Ghost turns, pulls me close, placing his hand behind my neck to tilt my face up, and slams his lips down on mine. It's a bruising kiss, but I'm robotic in my response, and I don't return it.

When the kiss ends, he stares into my eyes like he is trying to figure something out. His eyes are cold and so is his voice when he states, "This is far from finished Jez, and if I hear you call yourself a fucking freak ever again, I'll put you across my knee and spank your ass until it's red raw."

With that statement he releases his hold on me, turns, and walks away, heading downstairs.

That's the second time he has mentioned spanking me.

26

Since the epic failure in my bedroom, Ghost appears to be avoiding being alone with me, and only speaks when it's a necessity. He is civil, but doesn't speak unless spoken to, and most times his answer is merely a grunt.

Well, he can sulk as much as he wants to, but it pisses me off.

Just because I called a halt to us having sex, doesn't mean he has to go all sooky lala on me.

A few days after the non-event, Max asks to meet and talk with me alone.

We set ourselves up in the meeting room as we have on other occasions, and once Hope has brought us our drinks, we begin.

"What the fuck did you do to Ghost, gyal? He's been like a bear with a sore head since the day Sugar turned up dead. He disappeared with you, and when he reappeared he was so pissed off he beat the crap outta Slimeball for nothing." Max is looking at me perplexed.

"I did nothing to him," *That's probably what his problem is*, I think to myself, but I don't say that. "What makes you think it is my fault he hit Slimeball? He probably deserved whatever he got."

"Ghost don't go 'round just hitting people. He's been on a rampage since the day Sugar was killed." I suppose he hasn't told *dear old dad* he wanted to screw me, and it didn't work out in his favor. Or maybe he wanted to fuck me to forget she was dead for a minute or so. Thinking that could've been the reason makes me sad. Did he just want to forget? *Was* I something to take his mind off his old lady-to-be's death? It doesn't strike me that had been the reason behind my motives that day also.

"Well, when someone kills your old lady-to-be, it would piss off anyone," I retort sharply.

Max gives me a look I can't interpret, cocking his head to the side. Then he chuckles, "Oh, likkle gyal, she was never in the running to be an old lady, especially to Ghost. He is already taken, even I know that."

Wait.

What?

He's already taken?

Had I been tempted to sleep with a married man?

"Taken you say?" I grate through clenched teeth, my eyes narrowed and glaring, "Where is she? Who is she?" I am trying to act casual about it, but Max can undoubtedly see I'm pissed off.

He chuckles again.

"Oh, he's definitely taken likkle gyal. By the fiery president of the Broken Halos herself. None other than *you*, my Jezebel." He flicks the end of my nose lightly with his finger. "His heart belonged to you the moment he set eyes on you."

My eyes narrow. Max is not funny, although he's cracking himself up laughing.

"He doesn't even know me, so how can he be taken by me? Besides, who says *I* want him?" I hiss.

"He he heee, you should see your face, Jez. It's written all over it. The way you reacted when I said he was taken? You looked like you could cut a bitch." Max is full on belly laughing now.

Suddenly he stops, grasps my face in both his hands and looks into my eyes, his face deadly serious when he says, "He knows you better than you think, likkle gyal. Ghost is a mon on a mission, and that mission is to keep you safe, so you let him do his job, you hear me? Nothing upsets him more, than thinking he already failed you twice."

It's my turn to be deadly serious now. "What do you mean twice?"

"I cannot tell you certain things, Jez, trust me on this please. Ghost is here for you, and you, alone. No other woman is even in the race." Max must realize he's said more than he should and closes his mouth tight.

He changes the subject completely, talking about the week's events, the death and burial of Sugar, or what was left of her, the plans we have set in place to keep everyone safe and secure, but he won't be drawn out on what he'd said earlier, telling me I will be told when the right time comes.

As I lay in my bed that night, the conversation rolls around in my head like thunder in the clouds.

Did Max mean when we were coming back from meeting them in Nothing, and we were being followed?

When Ghost back-tracked to take out our unwanted company that got away? That was just the once though, so when was the other?

Despite my brain working overtime, I fall into a light sleep.

When I wake in the early hours before dawn, I don my workout clothes, grab my iPod and head to the gym again.

I work up a sweat on the pole, turning my iPod onto some heavy metal music to go with my mood, and go hard at it as the last few weeks' events run through my head like a bad C grade movie. I'm so worked up I probably would have kept going if I didn't spot movement near the entrance to the gym.

It's Rosie.

She stands in the now open doorway, hanging onto the doorknob and looking in hesitantly, as if unsure whether to come in or leave. Her hair is lank and unkempt, and she seems to have lost some weight. Most of all though, she looks sad.

Stopping what I'm doing, I slide down the pole, remove my earplugs and look at her enquiringly.

"Do you want something?" I ask her quietly, knowing she holds me responsible for her friend's gruesome death.

"N-N-No. I'm sorry. I don't…" Rosie turns away as if to walk out of the gym, but I stop her.

"Rosie, right? Do you want to use the gym? I can leave if you're uncomfortable with me being here. I've finished my work out anyway." That's a lie, but she looks so sad and I feel guilty for her being that way.

"N-No. That's not why … it's your gym … I don't mean. Oh God, I'm sorry, I shouldn't be here. Ghost said if I came near you he'd …" Her voice trails off. She's not making sense.

"Rosie, do you want something?" I repeat, folding my arms in front of me, trying to be patient, but failing miserably.

"I'll just go …" Rosie steps to the doorway, and for some inexplicable reason, I rush to the door after her. Grasping the young woman by the arm, I stop her in her tracks, but she doesn't turn to face me.

"Rosie, please tell me what you came here for." I'm not good at dealing with other people's feelings, especially sadness.

With a heavy sob-sigh she turns to me with tears streaming down her face.

"I need to know *why*? Why did you send my sister away? Why did you let her get killed?" The young woman is sobbing now, her small shoulders heaving, "It's her birthday today. She was all the family I had left. After Momma died from cancer, and Bobby got killed in Iraq, she was all I had. I just need to know why? Why? She wasn't the best sister in the world, but she was mine. She was all I had. I want her back. Why can't I have her back? Why did they do that to her? I just want her back." Rosie's legs give way, and I follow her to the floor, wrapping my arms around her as she cries in heavy, hiccupping sobs.

I know this pain.

I've felt this pain, and I've asked similar questions of those who had no answers for me, just as I have no answers for Rosie.

Holding her to my chest I rock her while she grieves, and whisper quietly in her ear, "I'm sorry Rosie. I wish I could take back that night. I did warn her not to disrespect me in my house, but she wouldn't listen. I wish I had handled it some other way. Those animals will be taken down, I can promise you that. As for family? You have the Satans Vultures. And if they turn you loose, you come to me. We will be your family, the Broken Halos." I don't know why I'm saying all of this, but it's more than likely the guilt of feeling responsible for the lone blood relative Rosie had left being killed because I threw her out of my compound.

Responsibility for her well-being falls on my head now.

Nitro finds us sitting on the floor, and as Rosie can't seem to stop crying, she helps me take the young woman to my room, where she is given a sedative to calm her down.

Later in the day, I return to my room to check on Rosie, as I don't know how long the sedative will take to wear off, and she genuinely has me worried. The other women have told me she hasn't eaten for days, and Slimeball has been forcing her to have sex with him even though she's grieving.

No wonder his name is Slimeball.

Opening the door to my room, I see Rosie sitting on my bed with one leg underneath her and her arm hugging the other.

All she has on is a pair of cut off shorts and a tank top with no bra.

My breath stills.

She has my box, and photos are strewn across my bed.

She's been poking around in my room?

She has no business *touching* that box.

No one does.

Moving at high speed I snatch the box up from the bed, shoving pictures back into it as fast as I can without looking at them.

I *don't want* to look at them, and I don't want anyone else looking at them.

"What are you doing nosing around in my things? This is none of your business, bitch. I don't give a shit what you're going through, you have *no right* to touch my things, especially this. Get the *fuck* out of my room," I snap at her.

Rosie's eyes widen, and she shrinks up against the wall, pulling her legs to her chest and wrapping both arms around them, as if she's trying to make herself smaller.

Don't look at them, don't look at them, I chant inside my head as I push everything into the box.

"I'm sorry, I'm sorry. Ghost came by looking for his wallet. He said he thought he dropped it in here. I found it under the bed. I saw the box and picked it up. I'm sorry, I know it was not my business, but then this picture of a little girl dropped out and I got all curious. Please don't hurt m-m-me," Rosie babbles, stuttering with fright. When I look up she has a picture of Marley in her fist, holding tight to it.

"Is this y-you?" Rosie asks shakily. "Why don't you want anyone to see pictures of you as a little girl? You were cute." She leans forward tentatively, holding out the photo as if it's a peace offering.

Snatching the picture from her hand with force, it tears.

"Oh fuck." It's the picture I had taken of Marley and

Striker the day they were killed, and now this nosy bitch has made me tear it.

My legs give way and I plop down on the floor. I don't even realize I'm talking at the start.

"It's not me. It's my daughter." My voice sounds robotic, like I'm on autopilot, flat and expressionless.

"Your daughter? Where is she? Is that her dad? Did he take her away?" *Fuuuck*. All those questions. Does she not realize I don't want to talk about this? The box was hidden for a reason. So I didn't have to think or feel.

"No, that's not her father. It's Striker. They're both dead. Car accident. Satisfied? Now get the fuck out." I'm using my, *don't fuck with me right now* voice so she will go, but Rosie either has more guts than I give her credit for, or she's plain stupid.

"Oh gosh,"

Gosh?

Rosie sounds sad as she apologizes again for snooping. "I really am sorry. I'm so sad about Sugar, I wasn't thinking. Your little girl was so pretty. What was her name?"

"Marley," I blandly reply, looking down at the two pieces of the torn photo now in my hands.

"She looks like she was loved." Rosie's voice catches and I look up to see she's crying. "My Momma always treated us more like her sisters than a Momma. She was so vain. Sugar looked like her, and Momma hated her for that. The cancer took Momma's looks from her before she died. She said it was our fault she got ovarian cancer. I always thought the one person who ever loved me was my Bobby. We were going to be married when he left the armed forces. When he got killed overseas, I wanted to die too, but Sugar wouldn't let me. She took me to the Satans Vultures clubhouse and kept me with her ever since. I know you hated her, but she was a good sister. Now they're all the family I have."

For some reason I don't stop her rambling confession. Maybe this is what she needs to start moving forward with her life.

She lets out a sigh. "I don't have anyone to talk to about Bobby anymore. Every day that passes I miss him a little less, but I'll never forget him, or stop loving him. I don't even have any pictures of him, anymore. Slimeball took them all and burned them. He tells me to get the fuck over it, and to spread my legs 'cos that's all I'll ever be good for, but I want more. I want a man who loves me, and kids, lots of kids. Slimeball made me lose my baby when he found out I was pregnant. He punched me so hard in the stomach. He doesn't want kids. I never told Sugar about that. She would have killed him."

"Slimeball killed your unborn child?" I look up from the floor in shock. I knew he was an asshole, but the man is obviously much, much worse.

"Yes. He told me he will do the same if I get pregnant again. I told him last night I didn't want to have sex with him anymore but he … he made me. He said it's not rape because I'm a club whore, and sex is my job. My boobs are so sore I can't even wear a bra today." With that comment she raises her tank and I see teeth marks in her swollen flesh. They're red and bruised. One of her areolas has been bleeding.

"Why didn't you tell Ghost or Lucifer?" That animal needs to be taken out I think to myself as my eyes track the path of Rosie's bruises.

Slimeball has made sure she can cover them with her

clothes, there are none on her arms, face, or legs. He's a smart man for a dumb ass.

Rosie pulls her shirt down and whispers, "Slimeball told me they don't care what the men do to us, that we're there to fuck them any time, any way they want."

I place the torn half of the photo with Striker in it back in the box, put the lid on it, and push it back under the bed, making sure it cannot be *accidentally* found again. At least until *I'm* ready to find it.

The half of the photo with Marley on it I slide into my bra, close to my heart.

I have something else on my mind right now.

After seeking out Nitro, I ask her to find Rosie other quarters.

Rosie keeps apologizing. I think she's afraid I'll send her packing like I did her sister.

I have no intentions of doing that, although I *am* angry at her for snooping.

She should be punished for her prying, but for now I think she is suffering enough.

Besides, I know someone who certainly needs punishing, and he's about to get exactly what he deserves.

27

MAX IS SITTING ON THE BACK DECK, SMOKING A SPLIT with Dingo and Heathen when I storm out the door.

"Whoa likkle gyal, what's got you all riled? Is it us smokin' the joint?" Max leans forward as if to put it out. "I didn't know it would upset you. I see your people smokin' from time to time, so I thought it would be okay you know?" He frowns at me.

"I couldn't give two shits about you smoking weed, old man," I spit at him. "I want your permission to kick someone's ass."

I am seething with anger, and I need a workout.

"Who? You fighting with Ghost again, chil'? Do I need to put you two in separate corners?" He gives a cheeky smile, and I wonder how much weed he *has* smoked.

"This has nothing to do with Ghost. I want Slimeball in the ring. *Now*. That motherfucker has a beat down coming to him like he has never felt before," And I am the woman to do it. "So yes or no?" Standing with my hands on my hips, I watch confusion take place through the haze in Max's head. "You know what? *Fuck* your permission. Tell him to get his ass in the ring now. I'll be waiting for him."

With that, I charge to the barn and begin warm-up exercises.

"What's this about you wanting to beat the fuck outta Slimeball?" The unmistakable gravel voice of Ghost's sounds from the door.

"It is none of your business. You and Max have turned a blind eye to that animal, but I won't. Get him in here. If he's not here in the next ten minutes he can pack up and get the fuck off this property," I snap at him, not even hesitating in my warm up routine.

Of course, someone would have run straight to Ghost to let him know I was about to give one of his men a beating he would never forget. I expected that, the same as I would have expected one of my people to let me know if someone was about to do the same to one of my own.

That's not going to stop me, however.

The longer I wait, the angrier I get.

"Jez, he has at least a hundred pounds or more on you. Are you sure you want this? Slimeball used to be a street fighter back in the day. Maybe think about this before you go off half-cocked." As soon as it comes out of his mouth I spin and pin him with a death glare.

"Go. Get. Fucking. Slimeball. Now," I grate through gritted teeth. "Don't make me say it again." Turning away from him I climb into the ring.

Tinker and Nitro enter the barn as I am shadow boxing, while bouncing around the ring on my feet.

'What's going on, Jez?" Tinker folds his big arms across his chest. He is around thirty-five, short in stature, maybe five feet five, slightly stout, but fit all the same. His chocolate hair is short and wavy. Grey eyes look up at me, studying my body language as he tries to figure out my mood.

When I don't answer straight away he asks again in his slow southern drawl, "What's put a bee in yer bonnet this time?"

Nitro is quiet, observing me.

Stopping for a moment, I copy Tinker's stance and fold my arms across my chest.

"No bee in this bonnet, Tinker, some much needed justice. It's about time Slimeball found out who is judge, jury and fucking executioner if needs be, in this compound." My voice is calm and quiet, unlike my mood. "I want the cage lowered when he gets in the ring, and it doesn't rise until I give the okay. Is that understood?" I look at both of them in turn.

Both have their lips pressed together, and I sense their struggle with my command. "*That* is an order." I'm committed to this, and they will not change my decision.

Nitro nods her head, but I know she isn't happy. "So, are you going to tell us why, Jez?" She knows he must have done something especially bad for me to be even considering this.

The one and only time the cage has been lowered since we took over this compound was after Striker and Marley left us, when one of Striker's club members decided he wanted to take over the Broken Halos' presidency.

He also intended to claim me.

That fucker is now food for the vultures.

"That's not my story to tell, Nitro." I allow my voice to soften. "Tell Rosie he won't be bothering her again. She'll be free to find someone who can give her what she deserves ... and kids." My voice tapers off.

I cannot get soft now.

"So, *cunt,*" I hear shouted from the doorway. I *hate* that fucking word. "I hear you have a problem you want to sort out with me in this little ring of yours. Speakin' of rings, that fuckin' little Rosie is gonna have a sore one once I finish with you. I hear she's been runnin' off at the mouth about me. Little cunt." Slimeball makes his way towards the ring, sneering.

There's that word again.

I grit my teeth.

As he draws closer, I can see the bruises on his face from his altercation with Ghost earlier. He thinks he has bruises now, they're nothing compared to the beat down I'm about to hand him. Placing both hands on the ropes of the ring, I look down at him from my position.

"You call yourself a man laying your hands on a woman who's not much more than a girl?" His eyes widen a little at my exposé. My lip curls and I sneer at him. "Let's see how you do against a woman who can fight back, Fuckwad." I use the nickname I gave him when we first met at the hotel. "No holds barred." I hold both my arms out, cocking my head at him, and give him a fake smile.

"All I'll have to do is touch you and Lucifer and Ghost will fucking kill me, bitch. You know it and so do I. It might be worth it though to cut you down to fucking size. I'm gonna hit you so hard, you ain't gonna know what fucking day it is." Slimeball removes his cut, then pulls his dirty gray T-shirt over his head and throws it to the ground. "I am so gonna enjoy seeing you beg, cunt. Afterwards *you* can be my bitch. I'll teach you what your smart mouth can be better used for."

Hearing the growl from the other side of the ring, I hold up my hand to silence it.

My eyes are narrow as I glare down at the animal calling himself Slimeball. "Get in the ring, Fuckwad and we will see *who* will be *whose* bitch," I reply calmly, not letting on how much I want … no … *need* to hit him.

As I wait for the smarmy bastard to remove his cut and T-shirt, and climb on into the ring, I hear Ghost growling from the opposite side.

"I can't let you do this, Jez, let me fight him. He's too big. He used to be a fucking fighter for God's sake. What the fuck did he *do* to get you so mad at him?" Turning to face Ghost, I don't say anything at first. I only stare at him with my head cocked.

Then I blow out a sigh, and he visibly relaxes. I think he thinks I'm going to give in and let him fight Slimeball. He drops down from the side of the ring and begins to remove his cut.

"Not. Gonna. Happen." Hearing the emphasis on those three words, Ghost freezes. "You all let him treat your whores like they aren't even human. You and … *Lucifer*." I snap the word with a sarcastic twist. "Well in my club, everyone is respected and treated as an individual. There is no way I would allow anyone in this club to get away with rape. Or being beaten into submission. Or being physically marked by another member without their permission. *Apparently,* the great Lucifer and his VP do, seeing as how they are merely *club whores.*" I use my fingers to show I'm quoting someone else's words. "They aren't human, according to your club members, so they can do whatever ... they ... fucking ... like to them. Well *not* in my house." Finished with what I have to say now, I stand with my feet apart and my hands defiantly on my hips.

I feel thumping of the floor and know Slimeball has finally climbed into the ring when I hear his snide laugh behind me.

"Okay, cunt. Let's sort this."

Glancing around the barn, I ensure it's the two of us inside the ring, and nod to Tinker.

He hesitates, but when I nod again, he hits the button and the cage lowers.

Slimeball looks up startled.

Ghost is cursing. He had jumped down from the side of the ring to rid himself of excess clothing, and now it's too late for him to get back up here, so he can't slip inside the ring.

The ten-foot-tall iron cage settles with a clank, and Slimeball chuckles.

He sounds a little nervous when he says, "Well, don't that beat all. There's no escape now, bitch, and no one to save you."

With that he charges straight at me.

At the last minute I step to the side, jump up and slam my elbow into his left shoulder blade as hard as I can, using every ounce of weight I have.

If I'm to have any chance at nailing him, I need to weaken his strong points fast, exactly like Lordy showed me. Slimeball was a fighter so his shoulders and fists are his strongest points.

Slimeball hits the cage and it rattles as he grasps it to stop himself falling.

"You're a slippery bitch, must be that skin of yours, full of oil," he snarks.

I know he hopes to rile me. He doesn't know how angry I already am, but he will.

"What the fuck is happening here? Ghost, why is she in a cage with Slimeball? Jezebel, what are you doing, gyal?" Lucifer sounds confused and angry at the same time, his accent more evident.

Keeping my eyes, and my body facing Fuckwad, I yell, "This animal has been raping your sweetbutts for God knows how long and you two," I wave my hand between him and Ghost, "have done nothing to stop him. He raped Rosie again last night. The poor kid is grieving the loss of her sister, and this fucker couldn't leave her to it. Have you seen the teeth marks on her tits? He drew blood for fuck's sake. And where were you two when she was pregnant and this *asswipe* you call a brother, punched her in the stomach and killed her baby? You two did *nothing*. How many other whores has he been doing this to? Or is this how you all behave? If it is, you can all get the fuck out now or I'll take you all down. Do you hear me?" I'm beyond anger now and I'm ready to blow.

"Slimeball? What the fuck man? Is what Jez is saying true? Did you do those things to Rosie and the other women? Let me in there, Jez. Open the fucking cage and let me in. *Now*." Lucifer's fired up. I chance a glance toward him and see his caramel eyes are like mine when he's angry. They change to a deeper brown.

Maybe he truly didn't know.

Slimeball now pipes up.

"You weak cunts and all your namby pamby fucking rules and shit. They're *whores*, Prez. They take whatever we fuckin' give 'em. Rosie needed to wake the fuck up. I don't want no fuckin' screamin' bawlin' fuckin' kid. She refused to have an abortion, so I did it for her. Her slut of a sister tried the same thing on me once and I did the same fuckin' thing to her. You'd think she would've warned her sister not to try it with me. The whores love it rough, even if they say they don't. Rosie is a *whore*, Prez." Slimeball reaches down and thrusts his groin into his hand as he grates out his statement. He thinks I don't know he's slowly edging closer to me, as he feels I'm concentrating on Lucifer's reactions.

"Did you know about this Ghost? Heathen, did you?" Lucifer's face looks like thunder and his voice has a deadly tone to it.

"He gets a bit rough every now and then with the whores, Lucifer, but they haven't complained to me about it. I thought it was consensual. I had no idea about Rosie being pregnant, or Sugar. Ooof!" Heathen's words are cut off as Dingo punches him in the mouth, and he goes down to the ground flat on his ass.

"You farkin' knew, ya prick. I can tell when yar lyin'. I should farkin' kill ya. No woman, I don't give two shits whether they're whores or not, deserve to be treated that way. *Evva.*" With that comment, Dingo starts swinging his boot at Heathen while he's on the ground still, stomping on his ribs and arms as Heathen tries desperately to cover his head, pulling his body into a fetal position. Heathen doesn't fight back. He takes the punishment doled out by the Satans Vultures SOA.

"Weak fuckers." Slimeball is within hitting distance

now. I can see him in my peripheral vision. "I'll show you how a woman should be treated. Once I've finished teaching this one a lesson, Rosie and I are gonna have a round or two." With that comment, he swings at my head, and although I'm expecting it and duck, he is faster than I thought and his fist glances off my skull near my temple, causing me to see stars for a second or two.

My legs buckle, and I shake my head trying to clear it, as I realize I'm now on the floor of the ring on my hands and knees.

I hear Ghost grate, "Slimeball, you fucker, I'm gonna fuckin' kill you when you get out of that cage. Don't you dare fuckin' touch her again. Get this damn cage up. *Now*." His voice low and threatening.

"Don't you *dare* raise this fucking cage," I call out.

On the left side of the ring Lucifer yells, "Stay in that cage, Slimeball, cos I'm next in and you are a dead mon."

"Not if I get there first," snarls Ghost from the right of me.

"You weak fucks would kill me over a piece of ass?" Slimeball swings his booted foot at my ribcage.

Rolling with the kick, I grab his leg, using it to slide, spin my body, and strike the back of his other knee with both *my* legs, knocking his out from under him.

I hear the rush of wind from his lungs as he hits the floor hard, but he instantly rolls away from me and gains his feet at the same time as I do.

His training seems to kick in and Slimeball begins to dance on his feet, back and forth, back and forth, his hands fisted and raised in a defensive position.

I can't let him land too many hits, as he is a big man. He may have let himself go over time, but he still knows how to swing, and a good roundhouse punch would finish me.

Slimeball throws out a jab or two, trying to persuade me to counteract so he can bring me close enough to do some real damage, but I duck and weave like Striker and Lordy showed me.

We pound on each other, sometimes with me landing a solid hit, sometimes Slimeball does.

We both have nicks and cuts on us, but little real damage.

"You don't remember me, do you bitch?" he snarls loud enough for me to hear him, but soft enough that those outside the ring can't. Some of the other members from both clubs have entered the barn now, a few cheering Slimeball on, others shouting for me to cave his head in. His voice is so low I can barely hear him above the din.

"From outside The Last Whiskey? Of course I do, *idiot*," I reply, as I circle him looking for an opening, wondering what he's on about. Does he think I suffer short term memory loss?

"No. Before that. In Las Vegas." Slimeball smirks like he has some big secret up his sleeve, and I hesitate, looking at him with a confused expression.

Taking the opportunity, Slimeball throws a punch, slamming his meaty fist into my cheek, glancing off my jaw, as I jerk backward a second too late.

It hurts like a bitch.

Stars are dancing in front of my eyes, and while they are, Slimeball gains the advantage, grabbing me in a sleeper hold. His breath is in my ear as he whispers, "I was there the night you were taken. You didn't see me in the back corner of the bar. The barman was paid by *me* to put that drug in your drink. Stupid bitch. You think you're *so* great. Sanchez paid me good money to give him the opportunity to grab you. You weren't supposed to get away. You won't escape him again though." All the while he whispers in my ear, my mind is spinning.

Las Vegas?

The drug in my drink was put in by Slimeball?

My mind goes back to the bar the night I was attacked.

Wanting to have a couple of drinks before I turn in, I find a bar not far from my hotel. As I enter, I notice it's a bit of a dive. There's a bar full length against the right-side wall, with one bartender, and on the other side are small round tables with cheap steel chairs around them. There aren't many patrons. One is at the bar, hunched over his drink, looking like someone rained on his parade, and there are a couple of women and men seated at tables scattered around the room, and there, in the back, in a darkened corner, it's him. *Slimeball.*

28

SLIMEBALL MUST FEEL MY BODY FREEZE AS I remember, and his cold laugh in my ear causes goose-bumps to rise on my entire body.

"That's not the only time I got up close and personal with you. Sanchez let me lick your pussy before he threw me outta that motel room. It was sooo sweet." He pulls tighter on my neck, cutting off more air.

"Why? Why did you drug me for him? How do you know him?" I gasp. My voice is growing weaker and breathier as he squeezes my throat harder, air becoming increasingly difficult to draw in, but I have to know.

"'Cos me and my brother were going to take over your little pussy club as well as Satans Vultures and turn them into something for people to fear, you little cunt. Somehow Sanchez found out about our plans and he made us an offer too good to refuse. With you outta the way we would be free and clear to do what we wanted with your weak pussy club. My brother couldn't be patient though. When he heard you got free from Mr

Sanchez, he decided he wanted you, too. Fuck knows why. Then when you got pregnant and had that brat, Crank made a different deal with Sanchez. You killed Crank, didn't you? He never came back after he told me he was goin' after the Broken Halos. What kinda *pussy* name is Broken Halos anyway?"

"You know what? More action, less talking, Fuck-wad. The more you talk the more I want to kill you." My voice is hoarse, and my stomach's churning at his words. I don't want to hear anymore, I want him dead. "Your *brother* was piss weak, like you. I enjoyed killing him. He cried for mercy, before he died."

I don't remember killing Crank, just the aftermath, but I know this will enrage Slimeball, and I hope it'll give me the opportunity to get out of the hold he has on my neck. His arm is tightening with every word, and he can either choke me to death or snap my neck in this position.

"You cunt, I'm gonna break your fuckin' neck for that." Cursing, he shifts on the canvas, and I use that to my advantage.

It's now or never.

Falling limp, I drop like a stone, surprising him, and when he bends over trying to lift me back up, tightening his grip again on my neck, I grasp his forearm with both my hands on the underside of his arm, so he thinks I'm trying to loosen his grip. Then, as if I'm exercising on my pole, I stiffen my body as I use the power in his strangle-hold to swing my legs up and throw them around his neck.

Thank the stripper pole for giving me core strength.

The shock and speed of my move causes him to

weaken his hold momentarily, and as I wrench my head free, I reach down his body and I hammer both my fists into his cock, while my vajajay is right in his face, and my legs are squeezing his neck.

Screaming, Slimeball goes down to the floor.

I roll off him and turn, kicking him in the face while he's holding his nuts, gasping with pain.

"Fucking whore!" he shouts at me as my foot connects with his nose and mouth, "I'll kill you." Spittle, blood, and teeth fly from his mouth, his eyes wild.

Out cometh the beast.

Slimeball doesn't seem to care now. I think he realizes he's a dead man.

Looking up at me with utter hatred in his eyes, he snarls, "Sanchez is gonna come for you again, and this time there will be no rescue 'cos all your fuckin' freaks are gonna be dead. I wish I could be there to see it."

"You won't be and he's not going to get the chance." I bend a little to put more force into my next kick.

The photo of Marley drops from my bra onto the floor. I had forgotten it was there. Slimeball reaches out and grabs it. *I don't want his filthy hands on it.* He holds the photo up to his face for a moment and scrutinizes it. For some reason, he begins to full on belly laugh.

In between, he says something that changes my life forever.

"You think about your kid sometimes? I know Sanchez is the daddy. I helped set up that whole fuckin' accident. Striker didn't suspect a thing, fuckin' sucker. *He* has her now. As soon as she's old enough he'll marry her off to the next in line to the throne of fuckin' drug kings."

Slimeball spits on the photo of Marley and I lose what little sanity I have left.

He drops the torn photo and holds his ribs now as I kick him again and again. I don't believe a word this lying sack of shit has said. Maybe he wants to die quickly, but what if…?

I stop and stare down at him, then up to the people who now surround the cage.

Some are yelling, some are cheering, others are content to watch.

Though I can see their mouths working, I can't hear them; all I hear are Slimeball's words, and they make my ears feel like they are bleeding.

I look down at him again, and I think he realizes he's said too much.

His eyes are swollen, his lips bleed and there's a tooth or two missing from his mouth. Some of his fingers are bent at odd angles, probably broken, from trying to fend off my kicks.

Straddling his chest, I sit on him, and I punch him in the face over and over. I feel the skin on my knuckles crack open and the crunch of broken bones. Whether they're his or mine, I don't know and don't care. Our blood mingles together, smearing the canvas floor of the ring.

A red haze has taken over and I can't stop, until …

Someone picks me up and restrains me by wrapping their arms around my chest and pinning my arms to my sides.

"Jez … Jez girl. Stop. You'll kill him. Stop." Ghost's voice seeps in slowly, and as the red haze fades from my sight, I look at the man whose face is now unidentifiable, and even though I see he's not conscious, I scream at him.

"Where *is* she? Where *is* she?"

"Jez, where is *who*?" Ghost has me pulled hard against him, my back to his chest, and although his body is warm, I'm freezing, goosebumps are covering my skin, and my mind's churning.

Looking around the room again, I see the cage is up. I hadn't noticed it was rising as I mutilated the animal calling himself Slimeball.

Did I give the order to raise the cage?

I don't remember.

I don't care.

What I do care about is him answering my question. I don't care about the fact I nearly killed him. I would do it again and again. He needs to be alive long enough to open his mouth and tell me where she is.

"*Jezebel.*" I hear my father's thick accent through the white noise in my head and lift my eyes from the bloody and battered body of Slimeball to see Max standing in front of me now, one hand grasping and lifting my chin.

"Jezebel, come back to me, likkle gyal." His voice is softer now, his caramel eyes are filled with worry, and there's a crease between his eyebrows. "Where is *who*, Jezebel?"

The adrenaline that had been rushing through my body is diminishing fast, as the words I never thought I would say, exit my mouth in a strangled whisper.

"He says Marley's alive."

My hands and legs start to shake as the adrenalin rush dissipates and my knees begin to buckle. I barely register a voice uttering "Fuck," as someone sweeps strong arms under my knees and my shoulders, lifts me up and carries me away. Instinctively I reach my arms around his neck and close my eyes as I inhale the scent of Ghost, feeling safe in his arms.

The last thought I have before exhaustion overtakes me is my baby could still be alive.

AFTERWORD

Thank you for reading Jezebel Found. Keep following Jezebel and the Broken Halos MC as they face a cunning enemy while searching for the truth.

There is more to come.

ABOUT THE AUTHOR

I'm a heap of country, mixed with a pinch of city, laced with a sprinkle of hippy, tossed with a shake of bogan. I'm a wife, mother, and animal lover. I'm a good listener and have an eclectic taste in music.

You can find my website.

I don't do newsletters ...yet, but you can follow me on:

Instagram
Amazon author Page

ALSO BY B.A. CHILDS

Broken Halos MC Series

Jezebel Found (Book 1)

Jezebel Undone (Book 2)

…and more to come

www.ingramcontent.com/pod-product-compliance
Lightning Source LLC
Chambersburg PA
CBHW020638260626
47157CB00008B/2808